GOAL-MINDED

by
Lisa M. Bolt Simons

Minneapolis, Minnesota

DEDICATION

To Abdiaziz: I will never forget that your first word was "friend." To my son's soccer team: You rewrote the record books in more ways than one. To my twins, Jeri and Anthony: So glad that I was a soccer mom times two.

ACKNOWLEDGEMENTS

Thank you to Alicja, Anthony, Mike, and Nicky for the soccer expertise, and thank you to Kuresha, my cultural consultant.

Edited by Ryan Jacobson
Game design and "How to Use This Book" by Ryan Jacobson
Cover art by Stephen Morrow

Author photo by Jillian Raye Photography. The following images used under license from Shutterstock.com: MSF (soccer player), Prov910 (soccer field), Val Thoermer (promotional photograph), and vasosh (soccer ball)

10 9 8 7 6 5 4 3 2 1

ISBN: 978-1-940647-20-3; eISBN: 978-1-940647-21-0

TABLE OF CONTENTS

HOW TO USE THIS BOOK

As you read *Goal-Minded*, your goal is simple: make it to the happy ending on page 150. It's not as easy as it sounds. You will sometimes be asked to jump to a distant page. Please follow these instructions. Sometimes you will be asked to choose between two or more options. Decide which you feel is best, and go to the corresponding page. (Be careful; some options will lead to disaster.) Finally, if a page offers no instructions or choices, simply continue to the next page.

EARN POINTS

Along the way, you will sometimes collect points for your decisions. Points are awarded for

A) confidence,
B) skill,
C) speed, and
D) teamwork.

Keep track of your points using a bookmark that you can cut out on page 157 (or on a separate piece of paper). You'll need the points later on.

TALENT SCORE

Before you begin, you must determine your talent score. This number stands for the natural ability that your character, Abdiaziz, was born with. You can get your talent score in one of three ways:

Quick Way: Give yourself a talent score of two.

Standard Way: If you have any dice, roll one die. The number that you roll is your talent score. (You only get one try. So if you roll a one, you're stuck with it.)

Fun Way: Get a parent or guardian's help (to make sure you're in a safe place where no one—and nothing—can be hurt or damaged). Turn an empty garbage can onto its side so that the opening is on the floor, facing you. Stand eight steps away. Gently try to kick a soft rubber ball into the garbage can. Take six tries. Every time you kick the ball into the can, you get a point. You only get six kicks, whether you make them or not. If you miss all six, that's okay. As long as you're a good sport and don't get mad, give yourself one talent point for trying the *Fun Way*. Give yourself one skill point, too. After all, skill gets better with practice.

YOUR STARTING TEAM

AIDAN KANE
outside midfielder

BRYAN ZIEGLER
striker

ISMAIL FARAH
offensive midfielder

ABDIAZIZ HASSAN
outside midfielder (you)

NOORDIN DOLAL
defense

JETT WATTERS
defense

JESUS MACIAS
defensive midfielder

DANIEL GRAMSE
goalie

CHASE GANNON
defensive midfielder

ZACH MAHON
defense

FABIAN PIMENTAL
defense

PROLOGUE

*Author's note: Do you have your talent
points yet? If not, please read pages 4–5.*

It's the first soccer game of the season. Your team, the
Greenville Kings, is playing against the Cannon River
Cougars, and the Cougars are up by a goal. Losing the
first game is not a good way to start.

However, you're used to it. The Kings don't have the
best record through the years. In fact, Greenville has
never won more than four games in an entire season.
But this is a new team, a new mix of players because of
school boundary changes. Anything is possible.

Bryan Ziegler, the striker, has already netted the
Kings a goal. But your goalie, Daniel Gramse, has let
two goals zip by him.

It's the Kings' throw-in. Chase Gannon lobs the ball
over to you. You take it up the side of the field, speed-

ing toward the net. You manage to slip by the defensive midfielders, but a defenseman slide tackles you in order to steal the ball. The Cougars shift the direction of the action and hurry toward your goal.

An amazing pass from a Cougar defenseman to an outside midfielder catches the Kings' defense off guard. But Jett Watters is one of the fastest sprinters at your school. He catches up with the mid and kicks the ball out of bounds.

"All right, Watters, good job!" yells your coach, Mitch Cox, or M.C. as the players call him. "Now, let's get a goal!"

Noordin Dolal throws in the ball to Aidan Kane, who dribbles it up the field. Under pressure, he passes to the offensive mid, Ismail Farah, who then directs a pass to Bryan.

Bryan loses it, but you recover the ball and pass it to Ismail. He tries hitting Bryan again. This time, Bryan takes control and dekes past a Cougar.

Bryan boots it with all of his might. The soccer ball soars too high, over the net.

With just four minutes left in the second half, the Cougars' striker passes to the offensive mid, who passes back to the defensive mid. You attack, sliding yourself directly into the mid's path. He tries to swing around your left side, but you kick out your leg and tap the ball away from him. He scurries to recover, but you beat him to the ball and knock it to Ismail.

It's a breakaway. There aren't any defenders between Ismail and the goalie. Ismail drives forward, waits for the right moment, and takes his shot, kicking the ball at the net. But the goalie catches it to prevent a score.

The goalie kicks the soccer ball as far away as he can, but the ball goes to your defenseman Zach Mahon. He finds an open area and starts running the ball up the side of the field.

Zach gets the ball to Jett. He passes it to defensive mid Jesus Macias, who takes it up the field and passes to you. You're close to the net with a pretty good look, but so is Ismail. Should you shoot, or will you pass to Ismail? What will you choose to do?

To shoot the ball, go to page 27.

To pass the ball, go to page 32.

As excited as you are about your story, you know that you have to get your homework done. There's no deadline for your story, but there certainly is for math.

Unfortunately, the problems look like scribbles, and you can't remember how to do them. You leave the cash register and step into your dad's office.

"Can you give me 10 minutes?" you ask. "I need to call Chase and ask about our math homework."

"You don't understand it?"

"Not one bit."

Your dad shakes his head and says, "I'll help you."

Oh, no.

Both of you return to the cash register. In between the *very* few customers, Dad explains the lesson. It takes the entire time you're working at the store, but you do get your homework done.

AWARD YOURSELF 1 TEAMWORK POINT.

Go to the next page.

The Kings' home game is against the Saint Peter Vipers, a team that has won every game this season. You try not to get nervous, but your stomach feels like it's doing flips. This team doesn't just beat you every year; they blow you out.

As usual, the Vipers get on the board first. Their striker fakes out Daniel and taps the ball into the left corner of the net.

At halftime, 24 minutes later, the score is Vipers: 2 and Kings: 0. You feel deflated.

M.C. says, "We were in the same situation against the Thunder, and you pulled out a win. Let's do it again." He doesn't seem nearly as optimistic this time. It's like he doesn't believe the words he's saying.

When the whistle blows, the Vipers quickly start an attack, but Jett is ready. He steals the ball and, instead of passing it, he dribbles up the left side of the field. He's so fast that the Vipers can't catch him.

At the edge of the penalty box, he fires a shot—it sails just wide of the post to the right. That would've been an amazing breakaway goal.

Ismail and Bryan attack next, but the effort doesn't earn them a goal. The Vipers' defense stops them before they even get off a shot.

Next, you try leading an attack with a strong pass to Aidan, but that play fails, too.

Jesus gains possession. He passes to Aidan, who heads the ball to Bryan, and Bryan kicks the ball past the goalie and into the net!

One goal down.

Not 30 seconds later, Ismail and Bryan rush the ball toward the Vipers' goalie. Ismail kicks an amazing shot that soars over the goalie's head.

Tie game!

The Vipers stay aggressive. They keep attacking your net, trying to score. The Kings' defense plays hard, and the Vipers never get a clean look at the goal.

With four minutes left in the game, the Vipers get caught holding Ismail. *Yes!* That means a chance for a free kick.

M.C. chooses to let Jesus take the free kick, and it's a good decision. Jesus kicks the soccer ball to the right, but the goalie guesses left. *Goal!*

Behind by one, the Vipers play frantically. To their credit, they never let up. They work and work and work. But when the game ends, the score remains Kings: 3, Vipers: 2.

"The win is great, gentlemen," M.C. says. "But we will not repeat this performance. Get on the scoreboard first, and stay ahead. A team only gets so many come-from-behind wins, and we might have used all of ours up already. From now on, we play the whole game—not just the second half."

M.C. might be angry, but you're thrilled that the team won again. You believe that the Kings could beat anyone in the state.

Your good mood lasts all the way home, right up until you see your dad.

"I must switch your time at the store," he declares, "from Mondays and Wednesdays to Mondays and Saturdays. Saturdays will be our busiest day."

That won't work. Saturday is when you help Cory with his soccer practice. Do you dare tell this to your dad and risk making him angry? Or are you better off doing what he says? Cory will understand. What will you choose to do?

To agree to work, go to page 50.

To tell Dad about Cory, go to page 57.

You know it's wrong to take a reference book out of the library, but you're just going to borrow it for a few days. You'll bring it back before anyone even misses it.

You lean over to Jett. "I need your help. I have to borrow this book."

He looks at you, confused. "It's a library. You have a card. Go up to the front desk . . ."

"Gee, thanks," you reply sarcastically. "But I need to borrow a *reference* book. So I need you to go outside and let me slip it through the window."

"Bad idea."

"Yes, I know, but I need it for a few days."

Jett shrugs. "All right, fine. Where do you want me to go, exactly?"

"There's a window in the children's section. I'll go outside, and you slip it through to me."

You try not to look guilty as you walk between the security gates at the door and into the cool night. You wish it were winter, only because it would be completely dark right now.

You skirt around the corner of the library and hurry to the window. It's not open.

You peer in and see Jett. He moves a latch one way and tries to open the window. It doesn't budge. He moves the latch another way. It still doesn't budge. He moves the latch back to the original position, and he pushes harder than before. The window reluctantly creaks open.

Jett slips the book out the window, but it drops to the ground before you can catch it. You bend down to pick up the book.

"What do you think you're doing?"

At the sound of a woman's shrill voice, you bolt upright, leaving the book on the ground.

"Nothing," you lie.

"That book was just dropped out the window. Don't tell me you're doing *nothing*."

Your parents are called.

So are Jett's.

Fortunately, the police are left out of it. But there will be service hours at the library. There will be payment for the book that got damaged when it fell. Worst of all, there will be no more soccer. You and Jett are both kicked off the team.

Go to page 75.

"Dad, if I don't practice, I won't get to start. Miriam will be home in 15 minutes. Please, let me stay. This is important to me—and my team."

Your dad checks his watch. "Fifteen minutes?"

You nod.

"Okay, your mother and I will wait for 15 minutes longer. Even with this small delay, we will be on time for our appointment."

"Thanks, Dad."

"I am very excited, Abdiaziz," he continues. "I was finally approved to buy a store downtown. When the sale goes through, you will work for me and learn about business." He smiles and waves you away.

The thought of working for him causes you to frown as you hustle back to the practice field. Instead of working for your dad, you'd rather become as famous and creative as Cade Garrett. He writes a series of spy novels, and he's your all-time favorite author.

Go to the next page.

Back on the field, M.C. has two drills going. Some players practice dribbling the ball up the pitch. Others work on their shooting skills. The coach invites you to join either one. What will you choose to do?

To practice dribbling, go to page 68.

To practice shooting, go to page 69.

2

FIRST WIN?

It's the second game of the season. This time, you're up against the Eagle Lake Bulldogs. After losing that first game, you're feeling the pressure. You have to win this one. You can't repeat the slow start of last year. And the year before that. And the year before that.

Although the first game didn't show it, you feel like this season can be different. The team has a new kind of energy to it, not like those previous years.

You sit with your teammates in one of the soccer complex's locker rooms, listening as M.C. talks about tonight's game.

He says, "Show me what you did in practice, and you'll get the win. Guaranteed!"

Within the first 10 minutes of the game, Zach trips, and the Bulldogs' striker takes advantage of the mistake. He gets a breakaway and scores on a great shot that sails just out of Daniel's reach.

"Shake it off," M.C. yells from the sideline.

The Bulldogs make another quick attack toward Daniel, but Jett and Noordin stop their progress. Jett steals the ball and sends it to Ismail, who passes it to you. You're pretty far from the Bulldogs' net, but no one else is open, and no one seems to be guarding you.

You strike a high, arching kick directly at the Bulldog goalie. You don't expect to score; you're just trying to make something happen—except the goalie is too far forward. Obviously, he wasn't expecting a shot.

The ball arches downward, over his head and just out of reach. It bounces into the net behind him.

Goal!

After halftime, with the score still tied, 1–1, Fabian nabs a loose ball and kicks it to Bryan, who squirts ahead of the defenders.

It's a breakaway for the Kings. He shoots and scores!

You feel a fresh surge of energy. Your teammates run around, cheering and slapping hands with each other. The Kings are fired up.

With 15 minutes left in the game, Fabian passes the ball to Chase, who passes it to you. Bryan darts toward the goal, but you outsmart the defense and dribble even closer to the net. You fake a pass to Bryan, and then you kick the ball toward the bottom right corner.

Goal!

You feel confident as you head into the last part of the game with a 3–1 lead. Daniel holds the Bulldogs out of the net, and the Kings seal up win number one!

Go to the next page.

That night, you're studying math. *Trying*, actually, but you can't focus. You're too excited, and your brain craves a creative outlet. You put your homework aside, grab a pen and paper, and begin to write.

Bud looked around the ballroom, assessing the situation: His wrists were roped behind his back, his shoelaces were tied in knots, and he was sitting in what appeared to be a mesh cage for large cats—as in tigers or lions. A piano dangled 20 feet over his head.

"Uh, guys," he said into the camera that was sewn into the collar of his shirt. "This isn't good."

At the other end of the video feed, Lacey and Q sat with a laptop in front of them and five smartphones scattered about. Together, they worked through the coding of an app that would open any electronic door. They couldn't see Bud's face on the screen; the camera just displayed the thick wire that held their friend and fellow agent captive. The video moved slightly with the rhythm of his breathing.

Q and Lacey were only a couple of blocks away—in a hotel room in San Sebastian, Spain. But they needed to finish the app before they could rescue Bud, and they were short on time. The Loyals would return for him soon.

* * *

After you finish the first scene, you stare at your math. It needs to get done. Since the business deal is going well, your dad is in a good mood. Should you ask him for help? Or will you do your math alone? What will you choose to do?

To work alone, go to page 70.

To get help, go to page 45.

Aidan is in a better position to score. Plus, it's not a good idea to try a move in a game that you've never even practiced. You trap the ball with your chest and control it as it drops to the ground. You quickly pass the ball back to Aidan. He kicks it hard toward the top corner of the net—and he scores!

But it's too soon to celebrate. There are 36 minutes left in the game.

The Eagles are relentless in their attacks, but the Kings' defense plays one of its best games yet. Daniel stops some incredible shots that make the home crowd cheer with excitement.

You, the other midfielders, and Bryan continue to bombard the Eagles' goalie, but the Kings can't get the ball into the net again. Even a couple of corner kicks don't get your team a goal.

With only eight minutes left to play, the home crowd grows even louder.

An Eagle player almost gets a breakaway, but Fabian is ready for him. He steps in front of the player and steals the soccer ball. Fabian passes it to Chase, who passes to you.

You dribble down the sideline and kick to Ismail, since Bryan is covered. Ismail shoots, but his attempt hits the post. At least your team is killing the clock.

When the game ends, the Kings players run over to Daniel and celebrate around him. He was definitely the star of the game.

You're so excited. You wonder if your team will lose another game this season!

Go to the next page.

You can't wait to work on your writing sample for the contest. You don't have to send your whole novel—just a few chapters. You're doubly glad that the math teacher was gone today; there's no homework.

Mom is making chicken and rice when you get to the kitchen. Surprisingly, your dad is home, too, working on something at the table.

"We won again," you tell your parents.

He looks up from his paperwork. "Well done. I'll have to attend one of your games soon."

"Yeah, that would be great," you say.

You want to tell your parents about the big writing contest. But is now a good time, with Dad's business getting started? You don't want to keep secrets from them, but your dad is so focused on your math. Plus, there isn't much to tell them yet. You're just sending a bunch of work that's almost done already. What will you choose to do?

To tell your parents, go to page 63.

To wait, go to page 54.

You're in a good spot. The goalie isn't in position yet. You have a clear shot at the net. You kick the ball hard, aiming toward the top right corner. The ball speeds toward the goal, spinning enough to make it curve.

It hits the post and bounces away from the goal.

The Cougars control the ball and kick it out of their zone. Time ends the game before your team ever gets another chance to score.

A loss to start the season. Definitely not good.

Go to page 33.

As desperate as you are to take this book, you know it would be stealing, even if you planned to return it. Instead, you'll just have to come back to the library a few more times.

You and Jett walk home together; his house is just a block from your apartment.

"Are you ready for the game tomorrow?" he asks.

"No doubt," you say with a smile, hoping that you can get any sleep at all.

The Thunder score first, after their striker makes a brilliant move around Zach.

"That's okay, boys," M.C. says, clapping his hands. "Let's go now."

The Thunder score again, this time on a corner kick, 10 minutes later. Shoulders slump as your team heads back to center field.

M.C. yells. "The game is not over!"

The Kings hold off Canyon for the rest of the half, but your team doesn't manage to score.

In the locker room, M.C. says, "If you want to change our record, get out there and do something about it! They're going to play, thinking they already have this game won. Let's start fast and put one in the net within the first 10 minutes. Can you do that?"

Eight minutes into the second half, Jesus kicks the ball, and it sails over the goalie for the Kings' first point.

A few minutes later, Daniel gets the ball up the sideline to Aidan, who kicks it to Bryan.

Bryan fakes a kick to the right corner of the net and goes to the bottom left. The goalie moves the wrong way and can only watch the ball roll in.

That makes the score 2–2.

When a Thunder player gets a breakaway, Jett once again shows his speed. He sprints fast enough to catch up to the opponent, and he kicks the ball out of bounds, stopping a chance for an easy goal.

M.C. claps and yells, "That's the way to do it!"

After a poor throw-in by Canyon, Noordin steals the ball and passes to Chase, who passes to you. You deke a defender and spot Bryan streaking toward an open area in front of the net. You kick the ball perfectly toward where he's going to be.

He doesn't even slow down as the ball reaches him. In one motion, he gains control of the pass, spins toward the goal, and kicks the ball past the goalie.

"Three!" M.C. yells. "Now let's put on the defensive pressure, boys!"

That's exactly what the Kings do. Your team proves to be faster and more skilled than Canyon. You keep the ball on their side of the field for most of the remaining time. They never even manage to get off another shot.

Back at home, you share the news of your team's win, and your parents congratulate you.

Then your dad shares his good news. "The papers are signed. I will take over the business in a week, and I would like for you to start working for me."

"But I'm super busy with soccer, and I'm trying to keep my math grade up."

"You won't be playing soccer as an adult, but you will be working. This is a good time to learn."

"Dad," you plead, "soccer is really important to me. Please, can we figure something out so I can work and still play on the team?"

He hesitates for a moment, squints his eyes like he's solving a math problem in his head, then nods. "If you work hard for two days a week—and keep your math grade improving—you can continue to play. Do we have a deal?"

You nod enthusiastically, "Yes, deal," although you aren't sure that you'll enjoy working for your father.

5

NEW JOB

At practice, M.C. has your team work on a few set plays. You review corner kicks and goal kicks. Then you practice two different plays for scoring on free kicks.

M.C. also has the team practice different situations for throw-ins. This takes up most of practice.

The last 15 minutes are for players' choice. You can practice dribbling the ball up the pitch, or you can work on your shooting skills. What will you choose to do?

To practice dribbling, go to page 40.

To practice shooting, go to page 41.

You're in a good spot. The goalie is out of position. But Ismail is even closer to the net. You pass to him, and he kicks the ball hard. It zooms toward the goal, spinning enough to make it curve.

The soccer ball hits the post and bounces away from the goal.

The Cougars control the ball and kick it out of their zone. Time ends the game before your team ever gets another chance to score.

A loss to start the season. Definitely not good.

1

MATH FAMILY

When the soccer ball heads toward you in practice, you trap it like a pro, pass it to Bryan in front of the goal, and watch him smash the ball into the back corner of the net.

"Nice job, Zee and Bryan," says M.C. "Those plays are going to win us some games."

Zee—that's your nickname. It's short for Abdiaziz Hassan. You play outside midfielder for the Kings.

You smile and high-five Bryan then move to the halfway line to watch the next set of boys run the same play. Your team practices hard. No one wants your next game to be a repeat of the first.

Unfortunately, now that your turn is over, an earlier talk with your dad creeps into your mind . . .

"You're getting a D in math?" he asks, the report card crinkling in his hand.

"Math is hard for me," you say.

"What do you mean, hard? We come from a family of mathematicians—from business owners to teachers. We are speaking generations of mathematicians."

"Dad . . ." you whine.

"Generations," he repeats as if you didn't hear him. "If you studied math like you play soccer, math would be easy for you."

"I'm trying, all right?"

"Do you respect the teacher?"

"Are you kidding me?"

"Why would I joke?"

He still doesn't get American sarcasm.

Your family has lived in the United States for nine years, arriving here from the Ifo Refugee Camp in Dadaab, Kenya. Your dad has slowly made his way from worker to supervisor at his factory job. He hopes to once again run his own business soon.

"We have much to prove in this country," he says. "You will bring your grade up, or you will not play soccer."

You feel your jaw drop open. You move it in order to say, "Soccer is like . . . the legs of our country, and it's really catching on in the U.S." You think to yourself, Besides, I want to become a writer, not a mathematician. *Your dad would really pop a bolt if you told him that. To choose not to follow in the family's footsteps? It's unheard of.*

"Now we live here," he declares. "And now you focus on education. Raise your grade."

You try to focus on one of the things you love best: soccer. You close your eyes and push the argument out of your head . . . except now you're distracted by a car horn that's honking. Over and over.

You look to the field parking lot and see your dad. He motions for you to come to him. You don't want to—practice isn't over. But you can't ignore your dad.

You look at M.C. and signal that you'll be back in a minute. He nods.

You hurry to the parking lot. "What's up, Dad? I have practice."

"Yes, I know. But I'd like for you to come home. Your mom and I have to meet with a landlord about a building downtown, and we need you to watch your brothers and sisters while we're away."

"Why can't Miriam do it?"

"She's not home."

You look at his watch. "She'll be there in about 15 minutes. I really need to stay at practice."

"I prefer for you to come home now, until she gets home." He keeps his voice steady, like what he's asking is no big deal.

But it is a big deal. Of course, you don't want to disobey your father. He's a very strict and serious person. But if you leave practice early, M.C. will not be happy either. He just might bench you and not let you play. Either way, someone will be upset. What will you choose to do?

To leave right now, go to page 72.

To stay at practice, go to page 17.

You're too excited about your novel. You can't help it. You need to work on it.

AWARD YOURSELF 1 CONFIDENCE POINT.

"Dude, you're just in a cage in the middle of a locked room," Lacey said. "Been there, done that."

Bud leaned back against his hands, so his body camera focused up on the piano.

"Oh," Lacey said. "Scratch that."

Bud awkwardly pushed himself back up to a sitting position. "I think I'm going to tell my mom that I'll never, ever take piano lessons again."

"Nice work with the optimism," she replied, "that you will *be talking to her again."*

"Why wouldn't I be?" asked Bud. "You have this under control, right?"

Lacey looked at Q. A small line of sweat was running down the side of his face. It was a good thing Bud couldn't see that.

"Yep," she lied.

Q ignored their conversation and stayed focused, working and reworking the code. Lacey watched him closely.

"You can't write that line," Lacey said. "That won't open the lock."

"Yes, it will," Q replied.

"No, it won't. You have to shift this line up," she said, pointing at the screen. "Otherwise, it's the wrong order."

He glared at her, the frustration showing on his face. "Lacey, I've had more code training than you."

"Go ahead," she told him. "Run it and see."

Q ran the program.

Lacey smiled widely. "See? I told you that—"

"Guys?" Bud interrupted. "Can you two focus on pair programming, so I can get out of this mess?"

Q inhaled and loudly blew the air out of his mouth. "Yeah, sorry."

"Where is the rice?" a woman asks.

You set down your manuscript and show her. The bag she wants is on the top shelf, so you reach up and grab it for her.

When you return to the register, your dad is looking at your in-progress scene.

"What is this?" he asks.

"Um . . . a story."

"For English class?"

"No."

"Why aren't you working on your math?"

"Because . . . I was working on that story."

"Is it for an assignment?"

"No."

"Then you need to work on math," he declares.

"Okay."

Your dad greets a customer coming into the store and then walks back to his office. You take out your math book and slam it on top of your manuscript.

You try to start working on the first problem, but the problems all look like scribbles. You can't remember how to do them. You leave the cash register and step into your dad's office.

"Can you give me 10 minutes?" you ask. "I need to call Chase and ask about this math homework."

"You don't understand it?"

"Not one bit."

Your dad shakes his head and says, "I'll help you."

Oh, no.

Both of you return to the cash register. In between the *very* few customers, Dad explains the lesson. It takes the entire time you're at the store, but you do get your homework done.

Go to page 12.

"I'll practice dribbling," you decide.

First, you and the others do a lap around the field. M.C. asks you to increase your speed as you circle two more times. Then you and the other players take turns dribbling the ball from midfield to the goal.

After a few runs, you all take turns as defenders and practice dribbling down the field under pressure.

You feel good about your ability to move quickly with the ball.

 AWARD YOURSELF 1 SPEED POINT.

Go to page 42.

"I'll practice shooting," you decide.

First, you and the others work on kicking the ball between midfield and the goal. Next, you all practice crossing and shooting at Daniel.

After about 15 minutes, you work on corner kicks. The last 20 minutes are spent on penalty shots.

You're feeling good about your ability to shoot the soccer ball.

AWARD YOURSELF 1 SKILL POINT.

Go to the next page.

After practice, Mom drops you off at Dad's new store. It's downtown, so there should be plenty of customers.

You walk in the door and find your dad at the front counter. You don't see anyone else. There aren't nearly as many aisles here as in the grocery stores in town, but you do see some familiar items: cereal, juice, baby food, milk, and more.

Several shelves have bags of grains, like barley and wheat. You haven't seen these kinds of bags before, so you look at where they're from: Minneapolis. Weird. You thought there would mostly be imported foods from around the world.

It's the same with the spices and even boxes of dates. They're all from the United States. The black tea, however, is from Kenya.

Another row features pots, kettles, and other housewares. There's also a small selection of women's blouses, dresses, and hijabs, as well as men's shirts. Rolled-up rugs stand in a corner.

You go back to the front of the store. Dad shows you how to work the cash register and also how to stock inventory on the shelves.

"Why is so much of this food from Minneapolis?" you ask.

"It's not. That's where the distribution company is," your dad says. "Follow me."

He shows you the storeroom in case you ever need to restock the shelves.

"I'll be in my office," he says and leaves you alone.

Only a couple of his friends and three or four other customers come in. But your dad hasn't gotten the word out yet. The former store only had clothing, so he needs to publicize the additional merchandise.

You brought your math homework and your novel. Your math will probably take an hour or so to finish, but you're also only a few pages from finishing the next part of your novel. The sooner you write it, the sooner you can submit your book to publishers. After all, it can take a long time—even years—to get a book published.

Should you write, or will you get going on your math assignment. What will you choose to do?

To write your book, go to page 37.

To do your math, go to page 11.

There is a lot of time left in the game, so you decide to take the safer shot. As you approach the ball, you stare at the left side of the net. The trick works, and the goalie starts leaning in that direction.

When your foot connects, the soccer ball sails to the center of the goal. The goalie reacts, diving in that direction. He's close enough to the middle that he's able to knock the ball away with his hands.

Bummer. Still 0–0.

As play continues, Zach passes the ball to Chase, who passes it to you. You dribble toward the net and take another shot. This time, the ball scrapes the top post and angles downward into the back of the net.

Goal!

The Kings' defense tightens up after that. You hold off the opponents, not allowing them to score before the clock runs out. M.C. was right about your chance to win—so now you celebrate another victory.

Go to page 59.

Dad just got home, and he's talking with Mom. As usual, he sounds excited about the business deal.

"Dad, I need help with my math homework. Do you have time to look at it with me?"

His smile fades, and he gapes at you for a moment—probably, you think, in disbelief. You can practically read his mind. *Math should be easy for you.*

"Sit," he says.

You open your math book with your notebook crammed inside. You smooth the notebook pages as your dad goes through the assignment with you. The lesson gets easier to understand after he shows you what to do, and the homework gets done quickly.

After your dad leaves, you go back to your novel. You're learning about computer science in school—and coding. Of course, coding is computer programming. It's writing actions that make computer programs work. It's how apps and video games are created. You love to use your problem-solving skills and imagination to write about the connection between symbols and actions in coding. In fact, it's so interesting that you've decided to center your book on that subject. The topic of coding is a perfect fit for a novel about special agents who go on missions all around the world.

* * *

After soccer practice, you notice that one of your teammates seems upset.

It's Cory Wagner, a backup outside midfielder.

"What's up, Cory?" you ask. "Is everything okay?"

He sighs, hesitates, then speaks. "I think I'm going to quit the team."

The news is a jolt. You open your eyes so wide that it almost hurts. Cory has been with you since you first started playing years ago.

"What? Why?" you protest.

"Because I don't get to play. The other guys are better than me. I get that. You all have skills that I don't, so I know I'm not going to see the field this year. There's no reason for me to stick around."

"Cory, you can think we have better skills, and that might be true right now. But you can get better, too. It just takes practice. Work hard, and you'll improve. But if you quit, you won't ever get better, right?"

He nods. "Yeah, I guess."

"Something is happening with our team," you tell him. "Call it a hunch, but we have the potential to win a lot of games."

"We lost the first game," he replies.

"Sure, but we won the second."

"That's not even the point. It's early in the season. It might be easier for everyone if I quit now—"

"Dude, you can't quit! We've got a lot of season left. I don't want to see you go, especially after playing with you for so many years."

He frowns and shakes his head. "Why am I not as good as the other guys?"

"I don't know. Why am I not as good at math as my younger brothers and sisters? That's just the way it is. But you'll get better."

Cory nods. "Maybe, I guess." He slings his backpack over his shoulder and picks up his water bottle.

You grab his shoulder before he walks away. "What if we had extra practice on Saturdays? Just you and me."

Cory stares at you. "Really? You'd do that."

"Yes," you say. "I could use some extra practice, too, and it'll keep me away from math problems."

Cory laughs. So do you.

3

FREE KICK

At home, your dad asks you to sit. "Buying the store is nearly complete," he says. "You will begin working as soon as the papers are signed."

"Dad, I'm so busy with school and soccer. I can work more in the winter, but can you keep my schedule light, at least for now?"

"I'll consider it, if you keep your math grade up."

"Right," you tell him, but your mind says, *Good luck with that one, Zee.*

Today's game is on the road against the Academy Knights, a team that almost always beats you.

"You played well against Eagle Lake," M.C. says. "Show up like that again, and we'll win for sure."

Neither team scores in the first half, but your team plays well. This year's Kings team is definitely better than in previous years. You're surprised that this new mix of boys has come together so quickly.

Five minutes into the second half, you get knocked to the ground in the goalie box, so you're awarded a free penalty kick. Everyone else gets out of the way while you stand with the ball in front of the goalie.

You only get one free chance to score. Should you aim for the middle, closer to where the goalie is? Or will you shoot for the bottom left corner? It's a tougher play for the goalie, but you also risk kicking the ball wide of the goal. What will you choose to do?

To aim for the middle, go to page 44.

To aim for the bottom left, go to page 58.

Although you've committed to Cory on Saturdays, your dad and his new business have to come first. Your entire family is counting on his success. Besides, you don't want to make him mad.

"Okay," you say. "Mondays and Saturdays it is."

You call Cory and tell him about your new work schedule, but you find that Sunday afternoons are open for both of you. You agree to practice together then.

You wish that you didn't have something going on every single day, but at least everyone is happy.

 AWARD YOURSELF 1 TEAMWORK POINT.

6

WRITING CONTEST

At school, your English teacher, Mrs. Meyer, keeps you after class. "Thanks for staying, Abdiaziz," she says, looking through a stack of papers. "Ah, here." She hands you a printout. "I know you love Cade Garrett's work, and I just found out that he's judging a young writer's contest. It's a national event, and the winner gets to meet him in New York City."

You look at Mrs. Meyer with wide eyes. "Really?"

As you study the flyer, she points to a date. "The deadline to enter is only a few days away, but I hope you have something you can send. I only wish I'd learned about this neat opportunity sooner."

"That's okay," you say. "Thanks for thinking of me."

"How is your coding story coming along?" she asks.

You smile. "It's awesome."

"Well, if you want someone to look it over, let me know. Meanwhile, you should enter the contest. I've seen enough of your writing to know that you can submit something good. Who knows? You might even win."

Go to the next page.

As you warm up for the second half of tonight's game, you can't stop thinking about the writing contest. In fact, you've been having trouble keeping your head in the game for most of the night. You have to concentrate. The Kings are playing an archrival, the Evergreen Eagles, and the score is 1–1.

As the second half begins, Bryan and Aidan work the ball toward the goalie. You keep with them. Aidan cuts in and out to avoid the defense. He passes to Bryan, but Bryan is under pressure and passes it back.

Now Aidan is under pressure. He kicks the ball over to you, but the pass sails high and your back is to the goal. It's the perfect chance to try a bicycle kick toward the goal: kicking the ball while practically doing a backflip. It's something you've never done before but always wanted to try. However, you can't see the net or the goalie, so you'll be shooting blind. Otherwise, you can gain control of the ball and send it back to Aidan. What will you choose to do?

To try a bicycle kick, go to page 73.

To pass back to Aidan, go to page 24.

This isn't the right time. You'll tell them soon . . . maybe after you send in your submission.

You take your backpack into your room and sit on your bed. You read through part of your work.

Within five minutes, the code had been written and tested. Now, Q and Lacey had to hope that the app would work on the actual locked door that led to Bud.

They opened their hotel room door and peeked out. No one was in the hall. They took the stairs to the lobby and hurried out the back door. They were sure that the Loyals knew where they were hiding. After all, the Loyals—an international terrorist group—had a lot of technology at their fingertips.

So did Q, Bud, and Lacey. They were only teenagers, but they had genius IQs. It also helped that their parents worked in agencies like America's Central Intelligence Agency, the United Kingdom's Secret Intelligence Service, and France's Direction Générale de la Sécurité Extérieure. Their parents started teaching them how to code when they were toddlers. The kids started with JavaScript, but they also learned C++, iOS, Python, and even some languages, like Hozta, that few people in the world even knew.

As they grew up, Q, Lacey, and Bud wrote websites, games, and even an app that tracked a certain isotope, or chemical, of any unsuspecting person who was offered and chewed a special gum. Now, those old projects seemed like child's play to the trio. When it came to coding, there wasn't much they couldn't do. Yet the Loyals were proving to be quite a challenge. It was as if the group had someone with the same abilities as the three friends.

Your first chapter is good. You decide to enter the first 20 pages, rather than picking from the middle of the story. The manuscript has a lot of action right at the beginning. It should draw Mr. Garrett into the story.

You go to the webpage with the online form, and you put in the basics: name, address, phone number, age. One field asks for a one-sentence plot summary. You write, "Three special agents are experts in coding, and they use their skills to combat a terrorist group."

You upload your 20 sample pages. Then you check your information once . . . twice . . . three times. All you have to do is press the "submit" button.

But you're so nervous.

Your cursor hovers over "submit."

Just click the button.

Yet this will be the first time you'll put your writing out into the world. What if you don't win? Your chances are slim, anyway. Why even bother? Or what if you do win? Will your parents—your dad—even let you go to New York City?

You close your eyes, bite your bottom lip, and press down. You hear the click. Then you lie back in your bed, nervous but excited. You're proud of yourself for doing this. You just hope that Mr. Garrett likes the story as much as you do.

Go to page 66.

You instantly feel butterflies floating around in your gut. Your father doesn't like to be disagreed with by his children. He was raised to do as he was told, no matter what. That's what he expects from his children, too. But you have an obligation to Cory.

You speak, but your mouth feels dry. You have to force out the words. "I'm sorry, but Saturdays won't work. I'm helping a teammate with his soccer skills. I promised him."

Your father glares at you for a moment. But to your surprise, his face softens. "It is nice that you help this other boy, but I need you on Saturdays. It is when the store gets most busy. However, if you and your friend can practice earlier in the morning, you may help him and work at the store as soon as you're done. Do you agree to this?"

You smile widely, relieved that he didn't get mad. "Yes, that sounds fair. Thanks, Dad."

AWARD YOURSELF 1 CONFIDENCE POINT.

Go to page 51.

There is a lot of time left in the game, so you decide to take the riskier shot. As you approach the ball, you stare at the right side of the net. The trick works, and the goalie starts leaning in that direction.

When your foot connects, the ball sails toward the bottom left corner. The goalie reacts, diving in that direction, but the ball slips past his fingers.

Goal!

The Kings' defense tightens up after that. You hold off the opponents, not allowing them to score before the clock runs out. M.C. was right about your chance to win—so now you celebrate another victory.

 AWARD YOURSELF 1 SKILL POINT.

Go to the next page.

You're working on your novel when Dad comes home. You stuff the manuscript under your math book. Although you've already finished your homework, you review the problems in case he comes into the bedroom you share with your brother.

He enters. "How is the grade in math?" he asks.

You take a deep breath. "D+."

Your dad actually takes a step back, as if your math grade is some sort of contagious disease.

"Let me explain," you say.

"Quickly."

"My teacher is two weeks behind in entering our scores. I promised I'd study more after that, and I have. My grade will go up when she gets caught up."

"We have a strong family background in math."

"I know. But my brain doesn't—"

"Then you must get help after school."

You nod. "Okay, I will."

"I want a paper signed by the teacher that shows you are attending every day."

"Teachers don't teach it. Other students do."

"I do not understand."

"Students who are good at math help students like me who aren't."

Your dad thinks about this for a minute. "A signed paper," he says and leaves.

"Ooh, you're in trouble," your brother teases.

"Be quiet," you say, pulling your manuscript out from under your math book.

4

LIBRARY RESEARCH

Practice today focuses on an attack play with you, Bryan, Aidan, and Ismail. M.C. also has your team work on corner kicks for the away game tomorrow night against the Canyon Thunder.

"I'm sure you don't need the reminder," M.C. says, "but we've won four games so far. If our team wins, it'll be the first time the Kings ever won five games in a single season."

You should feel extra motivated, but you're buzzing with nerves. You imagine the others are, too.

After practice, you stop at the library with Jett. He's working on science homework. You just want to do more research on coding.

You remember that a teacher suggested some web-sites that allow students to practice writing code. You go to a computer station and jump onto the first site, one that helps you to create a game.

Jett tries creating the game, too, and he's a bit better at figuring out which commands go in which order. In your book, Q will be the best at coding, but Bud will be the problem-solver and Lacey the most creative.

You check the time. The library closes in 10 minutes. You remember that you need one of the reference books that can't be checked out; you want to take a lot of notes, and there are great diagrams to study. If you take it with you, you can get a lot of work done quickly—which will give you more time to concentrate on your math homework. Of course, you aren't supposed to do that, so maybe you should leave it here, take more trips to the library—and hope you still have time to improve your math grade. What will you choose to do?

To take the book with you, go to page 15.

To leave the book here, go to page 28.

You don't like keeping secrets from your parents, and this doesn't seem like a big deal. There's no reason to keep it from them.

"Mom, Dad, I want to let you know something: My English teacher thinks I should enter a writing contest, so I'm going to do it."

Your dad doesn't look up from his paperwork. "Hm, a contest?"

"Yes, a famous author picks the winner."

Now, he looks at you. "How much does it cost?"

"Nothing, it's free."

"Good," he says "Best of luck to you." He looks back down and studies his paperwork.

"Yes, good luck," Mom says, and she begins slicing lemons again.

Well, that was easier than you thought.

You take your backpack into your room and sit on your bed. You read through part of your work.

Within five minutes, the code had been written and tested. Now, Q and Lacey hoped that the app would work on the actual locked door that led to Bud.

They opened their hotel room door and peeked out. No one was in the hall. They took the stairs to the lobby and hurried out the back door. They were sure that the Loyals knew where they were hiding. After all, the Loyals—an international terrorist group—had a lot of technology at their fingertips.

So did Q, Bud, and Lacey. They were only teenagers, but they had genius IQs. It also helped that their parents worked in agencies like America's Central Intelligence Agency, the United Kingdom's Secret Intelligence Service, and France's Direction Générale de la Sécurité Extérieure. Their parents started teaching them how to code when they were toddlers. The kids started with JavaScript, but they also learned C++, iOS, Python, and even some languages, like Hozta, that few people in the world even knew.

As they grew up, Q, Lacey, and Bud wrote websites, games, and even an app that tracked a certain isotope, or chemical, of any unsuspecting person who was offered and chewed a special gum. Now, those old projects seemed like child's play to the trio. When it came to coding, there wasn't much they couldn't do. Yet the Loyals were proving to be quite a challenge. It was as if the group had someone with the same abilities as the three friends.

Your first chapter is good. You decide to enter the first 20 pages, rather than picking from the middle of the story. The manuscript has a lot of action right at the beginning. It should draw Mr. Garrett into the story.

You go to the webpage with the online form, and you put in the basics: name, address, phone number, age. One field asks for a one-sentence plot summary. You write, "Three special agents are experts in coding, and they use their skills to combat a terrorist group."

You upload your 20 sample pages. Then you check your information once . . . twice . . . three times. All you have to do is press the "submit" button.

But you're so nervous.

Your cursor hovers over "submit."

Just click the button.

Yet this will be the first time you'll put your writing out into the world. What if you don't win? Your chances are slim, anyway. Why even bother? Or what if you do win? Will your parents—your dad—even let you go to New York City?

You close your eyes, bite your bottom lip, and press down. You hear the click. Then you lie back in your bed, nervous but excited. You're proud of yourself for doing this. You just hope that Mr. Garrett likes the story as much as you do.

AWARD YOURSELF 1 CONFIDENCE POINT.

7

EASY WIN

Before tonight's game, you read Cade Garrett's blog about getting writing rejections. They are as common as throw-ins in soccer. Writers can't give up. They have to be persistent—just like playing in a soccer game when your team is losing.

As much as you don't want to, you try to prepare for a rejection from the contest judges. Just to be realistic.

The Leafield Hornets are your opponents, another team that has always beaten the Kings in the past. But M.C. reminds you that the Kings are on a hot streak. So you might as well keep going strong.

Bryan starts too strong, though. He gets a yellow card for grabbing a Hornet's jersey after losing the ball while trying to score. It's about the only thing that does go wrong for your team. During the next attack, Chase heads the soccer ball in for a goal.

This begins a deluge of Kings goals, including one from you that tucks the ball into the far corner of the net. It puts the Kings ahead, 4–0.

As your team celebrates, you realize that Cory has been sitting on the bench this whole time. Should you ask the coach to take you out and play Cory? He's been working hard. He deserves a chance to shine. But there's still a lot of game left—plenty of time for Leafield to mount a comeback. Is it worth the risk? What will you choose to do?

To ask to come out, go to page 84.

To stay in the game, go to page 122.

"I'll practice dribbling," you decide.

First, you and the others do a lap around the field. M.C. asks you to increase your speed as you circle two more times. Then you and the other players take turns dribbling the ball from midfield to the goal.

After a few runs, you all take turns as defenders and practice dribbling down the field under pressure.

You feel good about your ability to move quickly with the ball.

 AWARD YOURSELF 1 SPEED POINT.

Go to page 19.

"I'll practice shooting," you decide.

First, you and the others work on kicking the ball between midfield and the goal. Next, you all practice crossing and shooting at Daniel.

After about 15 minutes, you work on corner kicks. The last 20 minutes are spent on penalty shots.

You're feeling good about your ability to shoot the soccer ball.

AWARD YOURSELF 1 SKILL POINT.

Go to page 19.

Dad just got home, and he's talking with your mom. As usual, he sounds excited about the business deal.

You don't want to bother him, and you don't want to see the disappointment on his face when you tell him that you're confused—that you don't understand this math assignment. Besides, you believe in yourself. You can figure this out on your own.

You take a deep breath, crack open your math book, and take out the notebook crammed between the pages. You smooth the paper.

As you get back to working the problems, you find that your focus improves. Although the problems in the book are still hard, you feel much better about the concepts. You manage to answer all the questions.

 AWARD YOURSELF 1 CONFIDENCE POINT.

After the math is done, you go back to your novel. You're learning about computer science in school—and coding. Of course, coding is computer programming. It's writing actions that make computer programs work. It's how apps and video games are created. You love to use your problem-solving skills and imagination to write about the connection between symbols and actions in coding. In fact, it's so interesting that you've decided to center your book on that subject. The topic of coding is a perfect fit for a novel about special agents who go on missions all around the world.

Go to page 46.

The last thing you want is to leave practice. But you have to listen to your dad.

"Hold on a sec," you say. "I have to tell Coach."

You jog back to the field, hoping that M.C. won't get mad—hoping even harder that this won't affect your playing time.

"Coach, I'm really sorry," you say to him. "My dad needs me at home. He and my mom are meeting a guy about a new business or something. I know practice isn't over, but I have to go. I promise I'll make up the time."

M.C. waves like it's no problem. "Family first," he says. "I get it. Just give me an extra 15 minutes every day for the rest of the week, and we'll call it even."

"Thanks, I will."

You pack your bag and jog to the car, where your dad impatiently waits.

Go to page 19.

This is a perfect time to try a bicycle kick because of the ball's height and your position. You hope that you score because it will be the highlight of a lifetime.

You jump, flip backward, and scissor-kick your legs. Your foot makes solid contact with the ball, and you see it fly toward the net. But that's all you see before you fall to the ground.

For a moment, you feel a sharp pain that knocks your head to the side . . .

You didn't realize that you had closed your eyes, but when you open them, M.C. is kneeling next to you.

"Hey, Zee, welcome back," he says, forcing a smile.

"What?" Your head roars.

"You passed out for a few minutes."

You try to process what he's saying, but it doesn't make sense. Your body hurts—mostly your head, neck, back, and shoulder.

M.C. asks, "Can you move your toes?"

You can.

"Can you move your fingers?"

You can.

M.C. says, "Good, Zee, that's good. I think you have a concussion. Hopefully, nothing else. An ambulance is on its way, so relax and try not to move. Okay?"

You don't say anything, but you feel tears come.

"Don't worry," M.C. says. "You're going to be fine."

When the ambulance arrives, the technicians put a neck brace on you. It feels like your body is on fire. You've never experienced so much pain before.

"I have to—" you begin.

They turn you on your side as you throw up.

At the hospital, you're diagnosed with a concussion, whiplash, and a dislocated shoulder. The doctor tells you to expect weeks of headaches, mood swings, and difficulty concentrating. There may also be dizziness, memory loss, and vision problems.

This is how your soccer season ends. You won't be able to write for several weeks, either. You wish you could code yourself a quick cure.

Go to the next page.

GAME
OVER

TRY AGAIN

Dad needs help, and you can give it to him. That's more important than any math assignment.

You pull up the website and begin creating a new page for your dad. You enter his name and the name of his business, as well as the other information Facebook asks for. You upload a photograph of the store and one of a Somali flag. Then you click the "About" button, and you write.

You write your dad's story, how he came to the U.S. from Somalia. You write about his family and about his passion for business. You write about his store, how it's stocked with all sorts of unique items for the home and for the family.

You review the page, correct a handful of mistakes that you find, and save all the changes. You take a deep breath and throw out some hope, hope that your dad will get a nice bump in his business.

 AWARD YOURSELF 1 TEAMWORK POINT.

You find your dad sitting at the table, but his chin is near his chest, and he's snoring. You gently shake his shoulder. "Dad?"

He wakes and looks at you. "Oh, yes, Abdiaziz. What do you need?"

You show him the Facebook page. "I made this for your business. If you get the word out about this page, people might look at it. Others who are on Facebook can find it, too."

He wipes the sleepiness from his eyes and studies the new page. He doesn't say a word for several long minutes. At last, he looks up at you. "You did all this?"

"Yeah." He doesn't like it. He's going to ask about your math homework.

He smiles widely and pats you on the shoulder. "This is great, son."

That night, you go to bed feeling proud and content. You dream about your coding novel.

Q and Lacey arrived at the building where Bud was trapped. Just as they opened the door, they saw two Loyals crossing the street toward them.

"Show time," said Q.

They walked through the door and shut it behind them. Lacey pulled a tiny sphere out from her jacket pocket. It was the size of a marble, and it fit perfectly on the door lock. She pressed it for three seconds. The sphere dissolved into the grooves of the lock, and the lock started to melt.

"Four minutes," Lacey said.

She and Q hurried down the hallway. They reached the massive doors that led to the cage, to Bud—and the piano. Q pulled out his smartphone and put it next to the electronic lock pad. Then he opened the new app.

"Three minutes," Lacey said. Her tone sounded calm, as if she were saying, "Here's your hamburger."

Q entered a passcode into the app.

They waited.

Lacey glanced down the hall. "We have one minute."

"We should still have two," Q said.

"But these Loyals are clever," replied Lacey.

The lock beeped, and the door swung open. Lacey and Q rushed inside and closed the door behind them, making sure to reactivate the lock.

"What's up?" Bud said in the middle of the room.

As if on cue, the piano dropped 10 feet closer to Bud. All three agents yelped in surprise.

Q and Lacey ran to the cage. It was padlocked shut.

"We can break open an electronic lock, but this lock could be trouble," Lacey said. Her voice sounded nervous.

Loyals began banging on the door.

The piano dropped another five feet. It dangled just over Bud's head.

He glanced up. "This is going to hurt," he said.

* * *

On Monday, practice goes very well. Everyone looks sharp, and the teamwork is better than ever.

The first state game is only days away—and so is the trip to New York. As of right now, you're still not allowed to go. But you wonder if your dad will change his mind.

You think about giving M.C. a heads up about the trip. But you wonder if that's a good idea. If you tell him, you're going to lose practice time and *playing time*—whether you go on the trip or not. If you don't tell him, he'll probably be mad if you do end up going. What will you choose to do?

To wait to tell Coach, go to page 138.

To tell him now, go to page 132.

The Spartans seem to work even harder. A mid fakes out Fabian and shoots. You barely stop the ball by knocking it backward over the net.

You glance at the clock: 14 minutes until halftime.

The mid that faked out Fabian storms at you again. Fabian pulls on the player's jersey, and the referee blows his whistle. He awards the Spartan a free kick.

Not good.

You ready your stance in the middle of the net. You move your feet, side to side, hands ready. You watch the shooter's body. He's giving himself away. He's going to kick it toward the middle.

He thumps the ball, and you stand in place, ready to block it. But the ball soars far to your left, directly into the net. Now you've let *two* goals in. The Spartans are ahead by one.

On the Kings' next attack, a Spartan steals the ball from Ismail and takes it up the side. He shoots the ball into the corner before you even have time to think.

It's another goal, and your team is down by two.

The confidence you felt at the beginning of the game had nothing to do with playing goaltender. Now, that confidence seeps down into the grass under your feet.

Your lack of confidence—and lack of skill—is even more obvious after you let in two more goals!

When the whistle blows for halftime, you want to dig a hole and hide in it—anything but face your teammates. You don't have a choice.

M.C. blasts the defense. You just sit there and look down the entire time.

The good news is that you don't have to play goalie in the second half. The bad news is that your team is too far down. They're never able to make up the five goals that you let in.

Now, instead of being proud of a second-place finish, you feel guilty about blowing the game for your town, your coach, and your friends.

Go to page 75.

You won the contest. You got your dad's permission. You're going to New York City!

 AWARD YOURSELF 1 CONFIDENCE POINT.

Mom offers you a small suitcase, but you prefer to use your soccer duffel bag. It says "Greenville Kings" on the side, and you want to show this off wherever you go. You're making a choice to leave your team for this opportunity, but you're part of the reason they're in the state tournament. You're still part of the team.

You haven't flown since your family arrived from Kenya so long ago. But you know what you'll need to pack. You put one pair of jeans on your bed, as well as two nice shirts. You'll also need your best shirt and tie for when you meet Mr. Garrett.

That reminds you to check over the information packet again. You read through it to verify when you'll be meeting Mr. Garrett on Saturday.

Wait. Is this right?

You're scheduled to meet with him on *Friday* night. All this time, you thought that the meeting was set for Saturday night.

You keep reading. Oh, wait, again.

You're scheduled to meet him on Friday—along with winners from the other age groups. On Saturday, you have a 30-minute session with Mr. Garrett, one on one. Your slotted time is mid-afternoon.

Well, what else will Mr. Garrett be doing on Friday night? The group meeting is from 5 to 7 p.m., during dinner. What if you ask Mr. Garrett to change his plans and have the one-on-one with you Friday night after dinner? Then, if you can arrange for the right travel plans, you could fly home in time to play on Saturday . . . assuming the Kings win their semifinal game.

But you are an invited guest. It might be rude to ask Mr. Garrett to change his schedule, just for you. You wonder if it would upset him. You certainly don't want to do that. Is it worth the risk?

How many confidence points do you have?

If you have 3 or more points, go page 126.

If you have 2 or fewer points, go to page 98.

You peek at Cory. He's slumping on the bench a bit, but you would be, too, if you didn't get to play. The two of you have been practicing hard together, and it's time to see how he does in a game.

You hurry over to M.C. "Coach, can you put Cory in? We've been practicing, and it would be great to see how he's doing."

M.C. looks at the scoreboard: 18 minutes left.

He nods and yells, "Cory, come here!"

Cory is on the field within minutes.

 AWARD YOURSELF 1 TEAMWORK POINT.

He's still not the best player, but you definitely think he's improved. He even starts an attack with Bryan and Ismail. Bryan taps the ball to Cory in the middle, and Cory chips it over another player to Ismail, who gets by a defender. It would be an assist for Cory, but Ismail powers a shot that misses the net.

A Hornets player tries to control the ball but loses it, so the Kings—Cory, actually—gets to run a throw-in play. He hustles to the sideline and calls one of the set plays. But when he throws it in, he lifts his foot just a couple of inches and gets called for the penalty. You shrug. It's a basic mistake, but at least he's learning.

A few minutes later, a Hornets player kicks the ball out of play. Cory and Chase both run to the sideline for the throw-in. Cory says something to Chase, and Chase runs back onto the field.

This time, Cory's throw-in is perfect. The ball gets passed around. You wish you were out there, but it's fun to see how crisp your team looks.

Cory receives a pass from Ismail. He spins and kicks the ball to the goalie's high left corner. It's a . . . goal? Did Cory really just score a goal?

Yes!

8

DIFFICULT SITUATION

The season is going by so quickly: only seven more games until the sectionals tournament. And only two more weeks until you find out about the writing contest. Actually, you only have to wait one week to find out if you're a finalist.

After school—and after math tutoring—you visit a few websites that offer coding practice. Even as you wait to hear about the contest, you want to keep working on your novel. In order to write a believable story, you need to learn as much as you can about coding. Each activity builds your confidence in computer programming.

Tonight's game is a rematch against the Academy Knights. The Kings only beat them by a single goal,

1–0, the last time you played. You imagine that this is going to be a tough, rugged, close game.

By halftime, though, you're proven wrong. The score is 3–0 . . . and the Kings are losing!

"What's going on out there?" M.C. exclaims. "We need to be better than this. I want this team to go far, to make some noise, come tournament time. That won't happen if we play like this!"

Go to the next page.

You think about how you can improve your game. You think about practice and the core of soccer that M.C. tries to teach. You think about the soccer games on TV and the best players around the world. And you think about coding.

You focus on your speed. In your head, you write the code "moveForward( )," and you zip past defenders. Next, you focus on ball handling. Lines of code could be "moveForward(10), turnRight(15), moveForward(5), turnLeft(25), and moveForward(5)."

If only soccer skill and speed came that easily to you. They don't. You have to work hard to keep improving. But which are you better at: skill or speed?

If you have more skill points, go to page 144.

If you have more speed points, go to page 123.

If your totals are the same, go to the next page.

Go to page 123.

If your dad isn't going to support your dream of becoming a writer, why should you support his dream of a successful business? Besides, he wants math to be your top priority, so the best thing to do is keep your math grade improving.

Dad is sitting at the dining room table, but his chin is near his chest, and he's snoring. You should probably let him sleep, but he's the one so obsessed with your math grade.

"Dad," you say, shaking his shoulder.

He opens his eyes and looks at you. "Yes, Abdiaziz, what do you need?"

You show him your homework.

"The first questions are review," you say, "and these were problems you helped me with a few weeks ago."

He looks them over. "Yes . . . these are correct."

Good. That means you can get back to writing.

Q and Lacey arrived at the building where Bud was trapped. Just as they opened the door, they saw two Loyals crossing the street toward them.

"Show time," said Q.

They walked through the door and shut it behind them. Lacey pulled a tiny sphere out from her jacket pocket. It was the size of a marble, and it fit perfectly on the door lock.

She pressed it for three seconds. The sphere dissolved into the grooves of the lock, and the lock started to melt.

"Four minutes," Lacey said.

She and Q hurried down the hallway. They reached the massive doors that led to the cage, to Bud—and the piano. Q pulled out his smartphone and put it next to the electronic lock pad. Then he opened the new app.

"Three minutes," Lacey said. Her tone sounded calm, as if she were saying, "Here's your hamburger."

Q entered a passcode into the app.

They waited.

Lacey glanced down the hall. "We have one minute."

"We should still have two," Q said.

"But these Loyals are clever," replied Lacey.

The lock beeped, and the door swung open. Lacey and Q rushed inside and closed the door behind them, making sure to reactivate the lock.

"What's up?" Bud said in the middle of the room.

As if on cue, the piano dropped 10 feet closer to Bud. All three agents yelped in surprise.

Q and Lacey ran to the cage. It was padlocked shut.

"We can break open an electronic lock, but this lock could be trouble," Lacey said. Her voice sounded nervous.

Loyals began banging on the door.

The piano dropped another five feet. It dangled just over Bud's head.

He glanced up. "This is going to hurt," he said.

* * *

On Monday, practice goes very well. Everyone looks sharp, and the teamwork is better than ever.

The first state game is only days away—and so is the trip to New York. As of right now, you're still not allowed to go. But you wonder if your dad will change his mind.

You think about giving M.C. a heads up about the trip. But you wonder if that's a good idea. If you tell him, you're going to lose practice time and *playing time*—whether you go on the trip or not. If you don't tell him, he'll probably get mad if you do end up going. What will you choose to do?

To wait to tell Coach, go to page 138.

To tell him now, go to page 104.

You must take advantage of this opportunity. You'll meet important people who can help to make your dreams come true. You can't pass this up.

When your dad awakens, you tell him of your new decision. Then you go together for breakfast. You try to make your own waffle, but it gets stuck in the black pan. Then you spill juice on your shirt. Your day is not off to a good start.

The organizers schedule a special tour of Artichoke Publishing, but you and your dad get lost, walking there. The taxi ride back to the hotel is expensive.

The rest of the day passes by in a flurry of meetings with people who want to discuss you and your story. None of the meetings last very long, though. At first, you're too worried about your teammates to talk very much. After you find out they lost the championship, you're too depressed.

You shouldn't have come. You shouldn't have stayed. You should have been there for your teammates. Now, instead of being proud of a second-place finish, you feel guilty about a missed chance to win with your friends.

Go to page 75.

AWARD YOURSELF 1 SPEED POINT.

Go to page 112.

AWARD YOURSELF 1 SKILL POINT.

Go to page 112.

The more you think about it, the less you want to let your teammates down. You decide that it would be best to stay for the state championship game on Saturday . . . assuming the Kings win their semifinal game.

 AWARD YOURSELF 1 TEAMWORK POINT.

You can't help but feel down, though. Meeting Mr. Garrett is a dream of yours. You grab the information packet and page through it, reviewing all the cool events that you're going to miss—like meeting Mr. Garrett on Saturday night.

Wait. Is this right?

You're scheduled to meet with him on *Friday* night. All this time, you thought that the meeting was set for Saturday night.

You keep reading. Oh, wait, again.

You're scheduled to meet him on Friday—along with winners from the other age groups. On Saturday, you have a 30-minute session with Mr. Garrett, one on one. Your slotted time is mid-afternoon.

Well, what else will Mr. Garrett be doing on Friday night? The group meeting is from 5 to 7 p.m., during dinner. What if you ask Mr. Garrett to change his plans and have the one-on-one with you Friday night after dinner? Then, if you can arrange for the right travel plans, you could fly home in time to play on Saturday.

But you are an invited guest. It might be rude to ask Mr. Garrett to change his schedule, just for you. You wonder if it would upset him. You certainly don't want to do that. Is it worth the risk?

How many confidence points do you have?

If you have 2 or more points, go page 126.

If you have 1 or fewer points, go to page 120.

No, it's not polite to ask Mr. Garrett to change his schedule. Plus, it's not worth the risk. How terrible would it be for the organizers—or even Mr. Garrett himself—to tell you that you asked too much, that you are no longer welcome to come? A nationally known author would never change his schedule just for you.

You arrive in New York City on Friday afternoon. A taxi takes you to the hotel. You're nervous about meeting Mr. Garrett. You don't want to say anything embarrassing. You're also nervous for your team. If they lose tonight's game after such a great season . . . well, you can't think about that.

At 5 p.m., you and your dad attend the big dinner. After the meal, Mr. Garrett gives a short presentation about himself and his work. He finishes by telling the finalists to mingle and get to know each other. Then he briefly finds each of you to shake hands. To most of the winners, he simply says, "Congratulations," and, "I enjoyed your story."

You talk to the other finalists for a little while but notice your dad nodding off. You two head back to the hotel room. That's where you hear the exciting news that your team won and is advancing to the championship game. You wish that you could be there.

In fact, you wish it so much that you can't enjoy the rest of your trip. Saturday passes by in a flurry of meetings with important people who want to talk about you and your story.

None of the meetings last very long, though. At first, you're too worried about your teammates to talk very much. After you find out they lost the championship, you're too depressed.

You shouldn't have come.

You shouldn't have stayed.

You should have been there for your teammates. Now, instead of being proud of a second-place finish, you feel guilty about a missed opportunity to win with your friends.

Go to page 75.

You manage to survive the rest of the half without causing any more damage. Your defense picks up in front of you, keeping the ball away for much of the time. You do face another four shots, but you stop them all.

You notice how well Cory is playing at your position. But you want to get back out there and score some goals. You glance over at Daniel on the bench. He has ice wrapped around his wrist. *Not good.* You blow air out the side of your mouth.

At halftime, you catch a bit of good news. Daniel's wrist is just bruised, and he feels okay. He'll be allowed to go back into the game.

That means you're back to outside mid. *Yes!*

Fabian accidentally knocks the ball past Daniel and out of bounds, so the Spartans get to try a corner kick.

A Spartan player goes to the corner of the field, while the rest of his team lines up near the penalty box in front of Daniel. You and your teammates guard them as closely as you can.

When the referee blows the whistle, the Spartan in the corner kicks the soccer ball. It's a high kick, and another Spartan tries to head the ball in for a goal, but Daniel easily catches it as if it were thrown to him.

Nice save.

A few minutes later, on another corner kick, a Spartan player outjumps Jett. He heads the ball past Daniel and into the net.

It's a great play. There's no way you would have saved that shot, either. You glance at the scoreboard: 1–2 with 31 minutes left in the game.

Attacks go back and forth without a goal for 15 minutes. You pass the ball to Ismail, who crosses it to Bryan. A Spartan steals it, but Bryan takes it right back. He speeds toward their goal. He runs so hard and so fast that you're sure he's going to crash right into their goalie. But he suddenly stops and putts the ball into the corner of the net with the outside of his foot.

Your teammates shout and cheer. Your fans go crazy. The goalie didn't expect that tricky shot, which makes it even better. The game is tied!

The Spartans get more physical. One player fouls and is warned with a yellow card when he tries a slide tackle into Noordin from behind.

The Kings attack again, and Ismail passes the ball to Bryan. He gets tripped just outside the box, but he gets the ball back. The referee doesn't call a foul, though, so Bryan keeps playing. He tries a chip shot over the goalie's head, but Bryan boots it too hard, and the ball soars over the net.

The referee calls foul after foul on the Spartans. You can tell that their players are getting frustrated. They expect to win. In fact, they haven't lost a game yet this season. But your team has a chance to change that.

A Spartan shoves you from behind for no reason. You don't even have the ball! The referee must not see it because there's no call. You feel a surge of anger, but you have to let it go. If you shove him back, you risk getting a red card—getting thrown out of the game.

Time is running out. The Kings need to score, or you'll have to play a "sudden death" overtime, in which the first team to score wins.

Focus, you tell yourself.

Time winds down. The second half ends in a tie. The teams get a five-minute break before overtime begins.

"Listen, guys," M.C. says. "You can win this. You're doing what you're supposed to do out there. You just need to get one last goal."

As you walk toward your position for the kickoff, you think of your novel.

They were out of time. The heroes needed to move fast in order to save their friend. Q opened his jacket and pulled out what looked like a multi-purpose tool. But there was only one tool inside: wire cutters. They weren't strong enough to cut open the lock, but . . .

He unfolded them and sliced a large rectangle into the mesh cage as quickly as he could. Q dove through the hole and began cutting his friend free.

"Hurry!" Lacey exclaimed. "That piano is going to fall any second."

Q glanced up. "That's not helpful, Lacey," he said.

The piano shook slightly—and then it fell.

Q squeezed the wire cutters one more time and then pulled his friend toward him.

Crash!

The characters would write code to make this game a success for the Kings. You imagine that they wrote a code for you. All you have to do is run the program.

Run.

Add together your talent points and your speed points. How many points do you have?

If you have four or more points, go to page 147.

If you have three or fewer points, go to page 140.

M.C. has a lot on his mind, but you have to let him know what's going on. You can't keep the secret from your teammates, either—you're too excited.

After you tell the other players, many offer you a high-five and a "Congratulations!" You can tell that they're upset you might not get to play in the state tournament, but you can also tell that they're happy for you.

Your teammates gather around the net to work on corner kicks. You walk to the sideline with M.C.

"What's up?" he asks.

"I won this writing contest," you begin.

"Cool," says M.C.

"The prize is a trip to New York City."

"Very cool."

"Yeah, except I found out that the trip is scheduled for this weekend."

He stops walking. "Ouch."

You stop, too. "I don't know if my dad will let me go. Right now he's saying no. So I'm not sure if I'll miss the games or not. I don't want to, but this is a once-in-a-lifetime chance to meet a famous author and learn a lot about writing. It's what I want to do when I get older."

He nods. "I understand. Soccer is a game, but this is your future. When is your dad going to decide?"

"I don't know," you reply.

"It's Monday. Our first game is Wednesday."

You shrug. "If I go, we wouldn't leave until Friday."

M.C. sighs. "Okay, I'll have to see what we can do in case you're gone. I'd hate to lose you. You're one of our key players. But you have to do what's best for you."

You hustle over to the team. M.C. reviews the set plays and makes sure that Cory understands where to position himself if he's starting at outside mid.

"Hey, guys," Jett says, breathing hard. "Sorry I'm late, Coach. The dentist had a small emergency before I got there, so my appointment had a late start."

"No problem. Jump in," M.C. says.

Jett looks at you. "Zee, I got Zach's text about your trip to New York this weekend. Cool!"

As practice continues, you realize that M.C. is now playing Cory more than he's playing you. It's a little frustrating, but you understand why.

When you get home from practice, you decide that you need to sit down with your dad and make a final decision. But he doesn't come home until late. Typical. It's always about him and his business. He doesn't even care about your interests—or your plans for the future.

You don't see him on Tuesday, either. He leaves on a business trip before you're up and won't be back until tomorrow. Doesn't he understand how important this is to you? Maybe if his store goes broke, he'll get that there are other paths in life, besides business.

You travel with the team to New Czech to play in your quarterfinal game. The Kings have never played the New Czech Goshawks before—and there's most definitely a reason why they made it to state. They're fast, they're talented, and they play hard.

Bryan manages to get you on the scoreboard in the first half. The Goshawks answer in the second after wearing down the Kings with some stellar passing.

The second half ends in a 1–1 tie, which means overtime. Emotions are tense. One mistake, one defensive letdown, and your season is over. You feel a nervous thrill, and you focus like never before.

You field a pass from Jett and spin it over to Bryan. He spots Aidan streaking open toward the goal. Bryan feeds him a perfect pass, and Aidan lets it fly.

Goal!

Game over. You celebrate wildly with your team.

Go to the next page.

You finally catch up with your dad on Thursday. He sits at the table with a stack of papers.

"Dad, I need to try this one more time. The trip to New York is really important to me, and—"

He holds up his hand. "Abdiaziz, enough. I do not have the time or the patience to continue telling you *no* about something that is already decided. You don't understand because you're just a child, but my store is struggling. If I don't find more customers soon, it will go out of business, and we will have nothing."

You feel the anger well up inside, and for a moment, everything looks red. You blurt out the words before you can stop yourself. "I hope your dumb business does fail. Maybe you'll get that there's more to life than math!"

He falls back in his chair as if you struck him in the face. You cover your mouth with your hand, but the words have already escaped.

You expect your father to stand and yell, but he does neither. He just sighs deeply then calmly says, "I see you do not yet understand the importance of business and how the world truly works. Therefore, you will now be working at the store with me every day. Your soccer season is over."

Go to page 75.

If you don't ask your dad to stop, he's going to get kicked out of the game. You don't hesitate. You run off the field, into the bleachers, and to your dad.

"Stop," you say, and he looks at you.

You switch to the Somali language and let the words spill out. "Please, don't do anything. If you get into a fight with this man, you'll be kicked out of here, and you won't ever be able to come back. Besides, what if you go to jail? What would happen to your business? This man isn't worth all that trouble."

Your dad simply stares at you for a moment. Then he nods. He turns and leaves the bleachers.

After your father is gone, the referee forces the other man to leave, too. You hear the ref say something about him being banned from attending games for the rest of the season.

For nine minutes, both teams play, but it's a different game now. The energy is gone. It's as if the players' cleats are smeared with glue. The game ends in a tie.

Although you're sad that your dad had to leave, you hope he'll show up at more of your games, especially when the playoffs start.

* * *

Today is the day: Finalists for the writing contest are going to be announced. You can barely sit still. You help your mom make sambusas—fried dough filled with meat, onion, and spices. Then you go and help your dad at the store.

When you get back home, you check your email. Nothing.

You come out of your room, trying to figure out something to do to take your mind off the contest.

Your little sister Sara yanks on your hand. "Take me to Kwik Trip."

You reply, "How do you ask nicely?"

"Please," she says and yanks on your hand again.

"You're going to Kwik Trip?" Miriam asks, seeming to appear from nowhere. "I'm coming."

"Me, too," says Abdullahi, who also appears.

You roll your eyes. Being the oldest can be a lot of extra work. But at least you have an excuse to do something other than wait.

The four of you walk to Kwik Trip, get ice cream cones, and go back home. You look at the time on the microwave. You only wasted 30 minutes.

You check your email, anyway.

Nothing.

You decide to research some more on coding, and you practice writing game codes.

You check your email.

You go to a few soccer websites and look around.

You check your email.

You even watch a few online math tutorials.

About the hundredth time checking your email, you finally get the message. You open it, read it, and can barely believe what the message says.

You're a finalist!

You can't help yourself. You run outside and do a backflip on the grass in front of your apartment building. Other kids "ooh" and "ahh" and ask how you did that. The adults sitting on the grass, however, just look at you like you're crazy.

You run back inside wearing the biggest smile of your life . . . and then you remember that it's not over. You're just a finalist. You're not a winner yet.

Now comes another waiting game. Will you be the contest winner? The chances still seem slim, but you never really believed that you'd even be a finalist.

Still, you've never wished for anything so badly before in your life.

Go to the next page.

The week passes slowly. At practice, M.C. seems to know you're distracted. He gives you something else to think about. "I want you to get some practice as the team's backup goalie. Just in case," he tells you.

Should you practice your footwork? Or will you work on deflecting the ball with your hands? What will you choose to do?

To practice your footwork, go to page 94.

To practice with your hands, go to page 95.

On Saturday morning, just before you sit down to check your email, your phone rings.

When you answer, a woman's voice says, "May I speak with Abdiaziz Hassan?"

"This is Abdiaziz."

"I'm Linda Davidson from the marketing department of Artichoke Publishing. We do Cade Garrett's books."

Your hands start to shake. Your heart feels like it falls into your stomach. You didn't win. They're calling to tell you the bad news.

"I'm calling to tell you . . ." she pauses.

Just get on with it.

". . . congratulations!" she suddenly exclaims. "Your writing sample was chosen as the grand-prize winner."

It takes you a moment to process the news. When it finally registers, you sit in stunned silence.

"Are you still there?" Ms. Davidson says excitedly.

"Yes, thank you." It's all you can think to say.

"Okay, yes, you're welcome." She sounds just a bit deflated. She was probably expecting cartwheels and screams of joy from you. "We'll be sending an email with all the information. Look for it later today."

"Thank you, Ms. Davidson." You try to sound as thrilled as possible. "This is really great news. I'm so very happy right now. I can't wait."

That seems to help her mood. "My pleasure."

It's time to fill in your parents on *all* of the contest's details—including the trip to New York. You gather your whole family at the kitchen table and tell them every last detail, from the plot of your novel to Cade Garrett to the trip to the Big Apple. You save the best piece of news for last.

"I did it," you say. "I won the contest. I get to travel to New York City and meet my favorite author."

You expect a smile and perhaps even a handshake from your father. Instead, his expression remains solemn as he shakes his head. "No, you will not go. Is this why your math grade is so low—this *writing*?" he spits it out, as if it's a bad word.

"No, Dad, it's not. Math is just tough for me."

"But you've been working on this silly story instead of doing math. Is this correct?"

You look down. "Sometimes," you mutter. "But I love to write. Math is hard, but writing is easy. I'm good at it, too. I won a national contest!"

"You will focus on math for business, Abdiaziz. There is no future for you in writing," he declares. "You will tell these contest people that you cannot attend."

"But Dad . . ."

"That is all there is to say."

He gathers a stack of his business papers and leaves.

After he's gone, Mom tells you, "I'm proud of you, Abdiaziz. I do worry about safety, though. New York City is such a big, busy place. When is this trip?"

"I don't know. I'm supposed to get an email with all the details later today."

"When you get more information, let's talk about this again. Maybe we can find a way to make it work."

"Thanks, Mom. And don't worry about me staying safe. You or dad would get to come with me."

Her eyes open wide. "Really? Your dad might like that. Just give him time. He'll come around."

Go to the next page.

When the sectional tournament begins, the Kings are the top seed because of your record of 13–1–2.

Over the course of the week, you defeat the Leafield Hornets, 4–1, and the Canyon Thunder, 2–1.

The championship game matches you against the Academy Knights. It's a cold and snowy affair, and you think that perhaps Mother Nature is telling both teams to chill out.

Most of the players wear stocking caps, and some even wear gloves. You're glad that you wore a long-sleeve shirt under your jersey. Huge flakes keep falling as you try to navigate your way around the pitch.

Fabian kicks the ball up the sideline to Chase. He looks to pass to Ismail, but a Knight is in the way. So he kicks the ball to you, instead, and you speed toward the goal with Bryan. You almost slip on the snow as you pass to him, but he manages to control himself and the ball before booting it toward the left corner. The goalie slips, too, but he steadies himself enough to deflect the shot with his fingertips.

As the Knights attack, Jett prevents the ball from reaching Daniel. He steals it and passes to Jesus, who gets tangled with the Knights' mids. Aidan comes to the rescue—or tries to, anyway. He slips to the ground and grabs his ankle.

M.C. hustles over to him as quickly as he can move on the snowy field. He asks you and Ismail to help get Aidan off the field.

"Cory," M.C. says, "you're in."

Cory smiles at you, and you both head back to your positions. The rest of the first half is the same slippery, sliding game with a few shot attempts but no goals. As the half ends, the Kings go to the bus to warm up, rather than huddle at the end of the field.

"I know the weather stinks," M.C. says, "but both teams are on the same field."

These words and the knowledge that your team is so close to making it to the state tournament seem to spark a match in the cold.

In the second half, the Kings mostly control the ball on the Knights' end of the field, pressuring them and their goalie for long stretches of time.

As the clock ticks down and with the score still 0–0, Chase passes to Ismail. He crosses it to Cory.

Cory fakes out a Knight defenseman and drills the ball toward the net. The kick is perfect. The ball escapes the reach of the goalie and slams into the net. *Goal!*

The Knights never manage a score.

Your team is going to the state tournament!

9

PLAY OR GO

When you get home, you can barely concentrate. The Kings are the talk of the town. In just one year, you went from the bottom of the standings to the sectional champions! The state tournament is just 10 days away, during the weekend of November 5.

You open your laptop and check your messages.

Cool! You have an email from Cade Garrett. You quickly read it, barely able to contain your excitement.

Wait. No way. That can't be right. You read it again. And again. And again. It says,

I look forward to your visit on
the weekend of November 5.

You hear the front door close. Dad must be home from his store. Your light is still on, and he finds you in your room.

"I thought you'd be happy with your win today," he says. "You look upset."

"I am. It's just . . . something else has come up."

"What is it?"

You take a deep breath. "You know that contest I won? I'm supposed to go to New York City. It's the same weekend as the state tournament."

"There is no problem. You're not going to New York City. Correct?"

"Dad, this kind of thing doesn't happen every day. It's a once-in-a-lifetime opportunity—"

"I said no."

You finish your sentence in your head: *And you have to come with me.*

"Life is full of problems," your dad adds. "My store isn't getting customers now because of a new store down the street."

You feel angry. You're frustrated. To be honest, part of you is happy to hear this news. If you're miserable, then he should be, too.

You wonder if Dad can read your mind. Or maybe you accidentally smile—because he suddenly frowns and leaves your room. That makes you feel guilty—so much so that you feel a need to help him.

You have a huge packet of math homework due on Monday. If you don't finish it, your grade will go down again, and then you'll be off the soccer team. But what if you use this time to build a Facebook page for your dad's business? It could help him to get more customers in his store. What will you choose to do?

To work on your math, go to page 90.

To build a Facebook page, go to page 76.

No, it's not polite to ask Mr. Garrett to change his schedule. A nationally known author wouldn't change his schedule for you, anyway. Besides, meeting him would still mean missing the semifinal game. You don't want to do that to your team. You'll just have to enter more writing contests in the future. Since you won this one, you're sure that you can win again.

Before you take the field for your semifinal game, you get a message from the contest organizers. They're disappointed that you're not coming to New York, and they share Mr. Garrett's disappointment, as well. But they wish you luck in your future writing career.

You can't get that message—or the event—out of your mind. The game begins, and you can't focus. You won that contest. You should be in New York City. You should be getting ready to meet Cade Garrett!

You mess up your team's plays. You move to the wrong spots and pass to the wrong players. You turn the ball over too many times to count. Two of your worst mistakes lead directly to goals for the other team.

It's the most terrible game you've ever played. When M.C. finally benches you, the Kings are behind, 4–1.

Even with you off the field, the Kings cannot pull it together. Your team loses the semifinal game.

To make you feel even worse, the Kings lose in the consolation game the very next day. You should be proud of yourself and your teammates for placing fourth in the entire state. Instead, you blame yourself for losing the most important game the Greenville Kings have ever played.

Go to page 75.

You feel bad for Cory, but your team is on a roll. You don't want to mess that up. Besides, since the Kings are up by so many goals, this is a good chance to practice footwork, passing, and shooting in a game situation.

You help Bryan in another scoring attack. You two move down the field, bouncing the ball back and forth past the Hornet defenders. You set him up with a great pass to the edge of the 18-yard box. His shot smacks the right post and misses, but it was a nice play.

After Jett and Zach stall a Hornets attack, the ball is passed to Chase and then to you. You dribble the ball down the field and decide to try an advanced move called the rainbow.

You use your right foot to drag the ball up your left heel. Then you lift your heel, sending the ball over you and the defender. But as you skirt past him, you feel his foot step on top of yours. Your body twists, but your right foot stays in place. Gravity pulls you down, and you land hard.

You hear a snap, and you feel it, too. You don't need a doctor to tell you that your ankle is broken, and your season is over.

Go to page 75.

Speed is your strength. You need to use it to spark another second-half rally.

Play resumes at a fast back-and-forth pace—just the way you like it. Noordin passes to Jesus, who gets the ball to Chase. Chase sends it to you, and you zoom forward. You don't worry about fancy or form, just speed.

You work your way past two defenders. Despite what M.C. always coaches you to do, you don't pass this time. Instead, you sprint past another defender and jet straight toward the net. No one can touch you. No one can catch you! You make your way inside the penalty area and kick the ball like it's on fire.

The goalie might as well be stuck in quicksand. Your shot is that perfect.

You score!

After a brief celebration with your teammates, you look over at your dad, who's cheering. You're thankful that he came to watch.

Six minutes later, Aidan scores on a pass from Jesus inside the box. The ball hits the post and bounces in. Just one more goal to tie.

You keep thinking *speed*. You keep thinking *fast*.

Go to the next page.

Daniel stops a shot, batting the ball away from the top corner. Jett recovers it and passes to Chase, who clears it to you. This time, instead of taking a shot, you see that Bryan is open and hit him with a pass. He traps the ball nicely but is pressured by a defender. He kicks the ball to Ismail, and Ismail powers a one-timer just over the goalie's head. *Goal!*

And that's a tie game.

As the players walk back to their reset positions, you hear a fan yell, "Get those immigrants off the field!"

You look over and see a blond man standing at the end of the Academy parents section with his hands on his hips. Since you're on the right side of the field, you're the closest player to him. You stare back at the man.

You've never heard the field this quiet. That's when you notice several Kings parents leering at the man, and one of those parents is your dad.

"What did you say?" Dad asks.

The man looks at your dad and crosses his arms. "They let immigrants on the field." He gestures toward you. "They need to get them out of there."

"Honey," a woman sitting next to him says. "Stop. Please, you'll only make things worse."

"I am not fooled," your dad says, his voice rising. "You use the word *immigrant* in hate."

"What are you going to do about it?" the man says. His arms come up, and his hands curve into fists.

Dad is a calm person, but this other man is trying to stir up trouble. Should you go to your father's aid? If you go into the bleachers, you'll be out for the rest of the game. Or are you better off ignoring the situation and letting the adults deal with this tense matter? Your teammates need you to help them win this game. What will you choose to do?

To go to your father, turn to page 108.

To stay in the game, go to page 136.

Okay, why not? You'll ask Mr. Garrett to change his schedule for you. The worst that can happen is he will turn you down, and you won't know unless you ask.

You start an email, explaining the situation with your soccer team. You ask if Mr. Garrett can change his schedule. You also apologize for the short notice.

To your surprise, the event organizers reply right away, saying that they'll check with Mr. Garrett.

Fifteen minutes later, you receive a phone call. The stranger on the line tells you that arrangements have been made. You'll meet one-on-one with Mr. Garrett on Friday night after the group gathering. So you'll be home in time for the championship game.

The voice on the phone offers a "good luck" and "I hope you win" before ending the call.

Wow. This is going to be the best weekend of your entire life . . . as long as the Kings win that semifinal game without you.

10

USE YOUR TALENT

You have about an hour to wait before passengers board the airplane to New York City. You can hardly sit still. You try to read one of Mr. Garrett's novels for the second time, but you find yourself reading the same paragraph, over and over. You're nervous about meeting him—and you're more nervous for your team. You hope the Kings can get to the championship game.

Dad starts talking a lot. He must be nervous, too. He tells you more about his business. You tell him about coding and writing. He eagerly listens.

"What if I keep marketing your store?" you say to him. "I can write ads and maybe even build a website. You know the business side of things, and I know the writing side."

"That sounds like a very good idea," he says, and then he surprises you by wrapping his arm around you. He's never done that in public before.

New York City is as big, as beautiful, and as busy as you expected it to be. There's so much to see that your neck gets sore from all the up-and-down, back-and-forth gawking that you do.

At 5 p.m., you and your dad attend the special dinner. You spot Mr. Garrett, and your entire body feels a chill. You can't believe you're in the same room as him. You can't believe you're going to meet him!

After the meal, he gives a short presentation about himself and his work. You should be listening to every word, but you know that the Kings are getting ready to play pretty soon. You keep looking at your phone, checking the time. You wish somebody on the team would text you and tell you what's going on in the locker room right now.

As Mr. Garrett ends his talk, he tells the finalists to mingle and get to know each other. Then he briefly finds each of you to shake hands. To most of the winners, he simply says, "Congratulations," and, "I enjoyed your story." For you, he adds, "I look forward to chatting with you in a little while."

At 7:15, Mr. Garrett invites you to sit in a corner of the hotel conference room, while busy workers clean all around you.

He takes a copy of your submission out of his briefcase. "Wonderful story, Abdiaziz."

"Thanks, Mr. Garrett, and you can call me Zee."

"In that case, you can call me Cade." He thumbs through your work. "I've made a lot of notes here. I like the characters and the plot. I just got picky about a few of the details."

For the next 20 minutes, Mr. Garrett—Cade—goes through your work, making both positive and negative comments. Overall, he seems very impressed, and he asks to read the entire novel when it's finished.

"You'll be the first person I send it to," you promise.

He smiles. "Good. There are going to be several great sessions tomorrow. I know that you have an important soccer game, but you could really learn a lot if you stay another day."

"I wish I could. It's the state championship."

He nods. "Well, few writers ever get to meet agents and editors like you would tomorrow. If you can, please stay." He looks at his watch. "I hate to say it, but it's time to go. I'm one of those old people who goes to bed early and gets up early to write."

You both stand, and he shakes your hand again. "I hope to see you tomorrow."

As he walks away, you're positive that you won't be able to sleep.

Your dad shuts off the lights. You just sit in the dark, staring at your phone, waiting for a message.

It isn't until after 10 p.m. that someone—Cory—finally texts you.

2–1

Is he kidding? What does that mean?

Who won? you reply.

You wait.

And wait.

And wait.

He's doing this just to torture you.

Finally, you hear the beep of a new message.

Us, of course!

You leap off the mattress and start to shout. But one glance at your dad, and you know you can't celebrate loudly. Instead, you dance around the room, waving your arms and shaking your legs. You can't help it. This has been the perfect day.

Of course, you soon realize that the wonderful news creates a new problem—and another decision.

Should you go back and play in the championship game, like you planned? Or will you take Cade's advice and stay? Only a real team player would give up a chance to meet book agents, editors, and publishers.

How many teamwork points do you have?

If you have three or more points, go to page 141.

If you have two or fewer points, go to page 93.

M.C. has a lot on his mind, but you have to let him know what's going on. You can't keep the secret from your teammates, either—you're too excited.

After you tell the other players, many offer you a high-five and a "Congratulations!" You can tell that they're upset you might not get to play in the state tournament, but you can also tell that they're happy for you.

Your teammates gather around the net to work on corner kicks. You walk to the sideline with M.C.

"What's up?" he asks.

"I won this writing contest," you begin.

"Cool," says M.C.

"The prize is a trip to New York City."

"Very cool."

"Yeah, except I found out that the trip is scheduled for this weekend."

He stops walking. "Ouch."

You stop, too. "I don't know if my dad will let me go. Right now he's saying no. So I'm not sure if I'll miss the games or not. I don't want to, but this is a once-in-a-lifetime chance to meet a famous author and learn a lot about writing. It's what I want to do when I get older."

He nods. "I understand. Soccer is a game, but this is your future. When is your dad going to decide?"

"I don't know," you reply.

"It's Monday. Our first game is Wednesday."

You shrug. "If I go, we wouldn't leave until Friday."

M.C. sighs. "Okay, I'll have to see what we can do in case you're gone. I'd hate to lose you. You're one of our key players. But you have to do what's best for you."

You hustle over to the team. M.C. reviews the set plays and makes sure that Cory understands where to position himself if he's starting at outside mid.

"Hey, guys," Jett says, breathing hard. "Sorry I'm late, Coach. The dentist had a small emergency before I got there, so my appointment had a late start."

"No problem. Jump in," M.C. says.

Jett looks at you. "Zee, I got Zach's text about your trip to New York this weekend. Cool!"

As practice continues, you realize that M.C. is now playing Cory more than he's playing you. It's a little frustrating, but you understand why.

When you get home from practice, you decide that you need to sit down with your dad and make a final decision. But he doesn't come home until late.

You don't see him on Tuesday, either. He leaves on a business trip before you're up and won't be back until tomorrow.

You travel with the team to New Czech to play in your quarterfinal game. The Kings have never played the New Czech Goshawks before—and there's most definitely a reason why they made it to state. They're fast, they're talented, and they play hard.

Bryan manages to get you on the scoreboard in the first half. The Goshawks answer in the second after wearing down the Kings with some stellar passing.

The second half ends in a 1–1 tie, which means overtime. Emotions are tense. One mistake, one defensive letdown, and your season is over. You feel a nervous thrill, and you focus like never before.

You field a pass from Jett and spin it over to Bryan. He spots Aidan streaking open toward the goal. Bryan feeds him a perfect pass, and Aidan lets it fly.

Goal!

Game over. You celebrate wildly with your team.

You finally catch up with your dad on Thursday. He sits at the table with a stack of papers.

"I found your story," he says. "It was in with your math homework. I read it, and it's good."

The thought of your dad reading your work makes you blush. "Thank you," you say.

"I also read my business page on Facebook. Many of my customers have, too—especially the new ones. Business has been good." He pauses, like he's thinking about what to say next. "I do not think a mathematician could have made that page so well. Only a writer could do that." He looks at your manuscript and back at you. "Going to New York City is important to you. We can go together, if that's what you decide."

"Dad, we'd have to leave tomorrow."

He smiles. "It won't take me long to pack."

You want to stay and finish the state tournament. You also want to go to New York City and learn more about writing. What will you choose to do?

To stay and play, go to page 96.

To visit New York City, go to page 82.

It's best to ignore what's going on in the stands. Let the adults handle it. There's nothing you can do.

As you continue to your position, you hear shouts and screaming. You turn to see men holding back the man who made the comment—and holding back your dad! The stranger and your dad are yelling at each other, even as they get pulled in separate directions.

The center referee runs over to the melee. "Both of you, out of here now!" he shouts. "And don't come back. You're not allowed at any more games. The coaches and the league will be notified."

A few of the other parents lead your dad out of the fenced-in field as you stare in stunned silence. You can only watch in disbelief as your dad walks to his car.

A whistle draws your attention back to the game.

For nine minutes, both teams play, but it's a different game now. The energy is gone. It's as if the players' cleats are smeared with glue. The game ends in a tie.

Go to the next page.

When you get home, your dad is at the dining room table. "You are done with soccer," he says.

"Why? I didn't do anything."

"I will not have you around such hateful people."

"Dad, people like that are everywhere. And that was only one guy. This is the first time anything like that has ever happened at soccer."

"I need you more at the store."

"Dad—"

He stands and walks out the door. The conversation is over, and you know what it means: You're done with soccer forever.

Go to page 75.

M.C. has too much on his mind. You really shouldn't bother him unless you get the okay to go to New York City. Unless that happens, the news doesn't matter. You can't keep the secret from your teammates, however—you're too excited.

"Don't tell anyone," you caution the other players. "M.C. doesn't know yet."

The team gathers around the net, and M.C. reviews the set plays for corner kicks.

"Hey, guys," Jett says, breathing hard. "Sorry I'm late, Coach. The dentist had a small emergency before I got there, so my appointment had a late start."

"No problem. Jump in," M.C. says.

Jett looks at you. "Zee, I got Zach's text about your trip to New York this weekend. Cool!"

Your body tenses. Your heart drops into your belly. You're afraid to look at M.C., but you turn your head slowly, feeling the eyes of an entire team upon you.

M.C. has his hands on his hips, and he's glaring at you. "Excuse me?" he snaps.

You immediately look down. "I, uh, was going to tell you. I'm not sure I'm even going."

"But there's a chance you won't be playing with us this weekend?"

"Yes . . . if my dad lets me go."

"You know we're playing in the state tournament."

"Yes, I—"

"Not only are you on the roster for midfielder, you're also a backup goalkeeper."

You feel your cheeks redden. "Can we talk about this in private?"

"No! We'll talk about it in front of the entire team because it affects the entire team. When were you going to tell me?" he snaps.

"When my dad told me I could go."

"And when is that going to be?"

"I don't know. He doesn't want me to go at all."

"But he could change his mind on . . ." he throws his hands up, "Thursday morning?"

"I guess."

"You *guess*. Well, I wish you knew because now I'm going to bench you, just in case you decide to abandon your team and go to New York. In fact, I don't want your attitude around at all. If you think you might quit on us—before the biggest game in this town's history—I don't have room for you. I hope you get to go on your trip because you're off the team!"

Go to page 75.

As Bryan leads an attack, you speed toward the goal. A Spartan blocks your path, but you glide around him. Another tries to grab your shirt and hold you, but you're too quick. He can't get a good grip.

In your excitement, you forget to watch where you're going. You move too far down the field, ahead of the defense and without the ball. The referee blows his whistle—you're offsides.

You hit your thighs with your fists.

A Spartan defender gets a free kick. He boots it to the Kings' half of the field. There's a scramble for control between a Spartan and Zach.

Zach's opponent gets the ball free and fakes out Zach. The Spartan is still pretty far away, but he shoots a high arching shot. It looks good—too good.

Daniel has to wait and time his jump. He extends his arms . . . hands . . . fingers . . . and taps the ball.

He doesn't tap it enough. The ball squirts past him, into the net.

You should be proud. Your team just placed second in the entire state. Instead, you feel guilty about blowing the game for your town, your coach, and your friends.

Go to page 75.

You can't quit on your teammates. You need to go back for the championship game. Win or lose, you have to be with them.

You write a note to Cade, thanking him for his time. You hope that he understands your decision.

"Zee's back!" shouts Ismail.

As you enter the locker room, the team surrounds you, slapping your hands and clapping you on the back. This is where you belong.

"I should be thanking you guys," you tell them. "You got us here today."

"We wouldn't be here without you," says Bryan.

As the team warms up, you feel ready. You're sharp. You're focused. You believe that you can win.

The Kings start strong against your championship opponent, the Rost Spartans. Aidan scores four minutes into the game.

1–0.

Sixteen minutes later, a Spartan steal leads to a breakaway with two of their players. Only Daniel stands between them and a goal.

As the Spartans attack, one of them gets too close to your goalie, and Daniel gets knocked to the ground. Play stops as he lies there, cradling his wrist.

M.C. rushes onto the field to check on his player.

After a minute, he looks at you and says, "Daniel's out. You're in at goalie, Zee."

"Great," you mumble as you throw a yellow goalie jersey over your green one.

The Spartans attack quickly. It's exactly what you'd do if *you* were up against a reserve goaltender. Their mids pass to the striker, and it's as if he's running the 100-meter dash. He zips around Ismail, Jesus, and Jett with some of the most amazing footwork you've seen.

Is it because you're the goalie that you notice his skill? Or is it because he's coming straight at you?

He shoots. The first shot you see hurtles right by your outstretched hands.

1–1.

You go into the net to retrieve the ball, and you take a deep breath. *It's just one. Just one. Let it go.*

On the next attack, two Spartans pass the ball back and forth to get you confused. You don't know where the shot will come from.

The defense tries to kick the ball out of bounds, but the Spartans move with speed and skill. All the action moves to your right, and you slide that way, too. But another Spartan sneaks to your left, and you notice him too late.

He gets a pass and shoots at a wide open net. You must be lucky, though. You dive to your left, and the ball bounces off the palms of your hands.

You've only faced two shots, and you're already tired and stressed out. You're not sure how much longer you can last in the net. Are you good enough?

Add together your talent points and your skill points. How many points do you have?

If you have four or more points, go to page 100.

If you have four or fewer points, go to page 80.

You're one of the most skilled players on the team. You need to use it to spark another second-half rally.

Play resumes at a fast back-and-forth pace. Noordin passes to Jesus, who gets the ball to Chase. Chase sends it to you, and you move forward with precise cutting and controlling actions. Your form is flawless.

You work your way past two defenders. Despite what M.C. always coaches you to do, you don't pass this time. Instead, you spin past another defender and glide straight toward the net. No one can stop you. Your skill is too great. You make your way inside the penalty area and kick the ball like it's on fire.

The goalie might as well be stuck in quicksand. Your shot is that perfect.

You score!

After a brief celebration with your teammates, you look over at your dad, who's cheering. You're thankful that he came to watch.

Six minutes later, Aidan scores on a pass from Jesus inside the box. The ball hits the post and bounces in. Just one more goal to tie.

You keep thinking *skill*. You keep thinking *control*.

Go to the next page.

Daniel stops a shot, batting the ball away from the top corner. Jett recovers it and passes to Chase, who clears it to you. This time, instead of taking a shot, you see that Bryan is open and hit him with a pass. He traps the ball nicely but is pressured by a defender. He kicks the ball to Ismail, and Ismail powers a one-timer just over the goalie's head. *Goal!*

And that's a tie game.

As the players walk back to their reset positions, you hear a fan yell, "Get those immigrants off the field!"

You look over and see a blond man standing at the end of the Academy parents section with his hands on his hips. Since you're on the right side of the field, you're the closest player to him. You stare back at the man.

You've never heard the field this quiet. That's when you notice several Kings parents leering at the man, and one of those parents is your dad.

"What did you say?" Dad asks.

The man looks at your dad and crosses his arms. "They let immigrants on the field." He gestures toward you. "They need to get them out of there."

"Honey," a woman sitting next to him says. "Stop. Please, you'll only make things worse."

"I am not fooled," your dad says, his voice rising. "You use the word *immigrant* in hate."

"What are you going to do about it?" the man says. His arms come up, and his hands curve into fists.

Dad is a calm person, but this other man is trying to stir up trouble. Should you go to your father's aid? If you go into the bleachers, you'll be out for the rest of the game. Or are you better off ignoring the situation and letting the adults deal with this tense matter? Your teammates need you to help them win this game. What will you choose to do?

To go to your father, turn to page 108.

To stay in the game, go to page 136.

As Bryan leads an attack, you speed toward the goal. A Spartan blocks your path, but you glide around him. Another tries to grab your shirt and hold you, but you're too quick. He can't get a good grip on you.

Everyone else on the field seems tired, but you feel fresh—like it's the first minute of the game. You even have to slow down to make sure you're not offsides.

Bryan kicks the ball to you. You control it and then go. Your burst of speed and solid footwork put you alone in front of the net. Only the goalie stands between you and victory.

You shoot . . . but the goalie knocks it away.

Bryan beats the Spartan players to the rebound, and he tries a shot. It hits the post and bounces straight to you. Quick as lightning, your foot connects with the ball and changes its direction. The soccer ball soars into the left corner of the net before the goalie even realizes what happened.

Goal!

Your town has done it. Your team has done it. You've done it. The Greenville Kings are the state champions!

EPILOGUE

"That was close," said Bud, as he crawled out the cage.

"You're telling me," Q answered.

"Don't congratulate yourselves yet," said Lacey. "We're not out of this mess . . . but I'm glad you guys are alive."

Q led the trio to a back window. He looked out and saw five Loyals guarding the back alley. "We can't go this way," he said.

He hurried to the main door. "We'll hide right here, against the wall. When the Loyals rush in, they'll run right past us. We'll run out behind them and up the stairs. We'll escape on the roof."

"I sure hope this works," said Lacey.

Q just looked at her and shrugged.

Your writing and coding skills have done the trick, or at least they've helped. Your dad enjoys a steady flow of customers at his store. You officially work part-time as his marketing manager now.

When you have extra time, you work on a new novel: a sequel adventure for Q, Lacey, and Bud.

After finishing your first story, you sent it to Cade Garrett. But he never wrote back.

Until today.

Zee,

I'll be in town next month for an author talk at your library. I'd love to take your family out for dinner. I read your book. I know a publisher who might be interested. Let me know if this works.

Wow. In a month you'll have a solid start on your new novel to share with him. You'll also be able to tell him the story of how the Greenville Kings became state soccer champions.

Go to the next page.

YOU
WIN

CONGRATULATIONS!

CHOOSE TO WIN!

Read the fast-paced, action-packed stories. Make the right choices. Find your way to the "winning" ending!

Goal-Minded
Out at Home
Save the Season!

YOU'RE THE MAIN CHARACTER. YOU MAKE THE CHOICES.
CAN YOU SURVIVE?

20,000 Leagues Under the Sea
Adventures of Perseus
Adventures of Sherlock Holmes
Call of the Wild
Dracula
King Solomon's Mines
Merry Adventures of Robin Hood
Three Musketeers
Treasure Island
Twelve Labors of Hercules

Enjoy a sample excerpt from Out a Home:

School's Out

Spring zips by. The Cardinals' record is an amazing 7–1 when June begins. What seems like all of a sudden, school is out for the summer.

Of course, when it comes to baseball, summer is what the season is all about. You and Puff practice more and more, in between exploring, adventures, and sleepovers. When Puff can't hang out, J.T. usually can. You were worried about him at first, but you're glad he moved here. He's one of your best friends.

Things at home are going well, too. The house is still clean, and your parents are staying out of trouble. Your dad has a job doing cement and rock work. Your mom enters information in the computer, working from home part-time.

June 4 is a game against one of your team's biggest rivals: the Red Earth Rams. Two years ago, they beat you. Last year, you came back to win. They're probably out for a revenge win this year.

The coach starts you at shortstop again. So far, you've started every game but one. J.T. stands by the bench and high-fives the whole team as they rush onto the field. Your dad is working today, but your mom and brothers are in the bleachers.

The first hit floats right to you, and you catch it with ease. Ever since that first game, you've been practicing with Puff, J.T., and also your dad.

Red Earth manages to score a run before the top of the inning is over. Since it's only one, you're sure that your team will come back.

You get a single in the bottom of the inning, but Puff strikes out to end the Cardinals at bat.

Back to the field you go.

The first batter smacks a foul ball that almost hits your brother Andy in the head. "Whoa!" you hear him say, even this far away from him. "That was cool!"

You shake your head.

The batter works the count to three balls and two strikes. Logan pitches, the batter swings, and something screams directly toward you. It isn't the ball, though.

You'd be ready for that. It takes a moment for your brain to register—the bat.

Just in time, you twist your body so the bat doesn't drill you square in the chest. But you still hear a faint *thunk*. You fall to your knees . . .

You are five years old. Mommy is downstairs, doing laundry. You want to show her the color graph you made in kindergarten today. You're so excited that she's home to show her. She's been gone a lot.

You're paying such close attention to your sheet that you miss the first step. You tumble down the stairs, land just the right way, and snap *goes a bone.*

At the emergency room, you learn that it's a collarbone. Your fingers find it and feel the bump. You have surgery. You wear a sling for six weeks. Each day, the purple fades; the bump is barely there.

A week later, your mom is gone again. Your dad has also disappeared. You and your brothers move in with a foster family.

Your fingers reach for your collarbone. You don't feel a bump. You didn't hear a snap. How did the bat find the same bone that you broke years ago?

Your heart is knocking on your ribs. You look at the bleachers to see your mom standing, her hands on her hips. Your brothers are standing at the fence behind home plate, gripping the metal, their noses sticking through the diamond-shaped openings. An umpire asks if you're okay, and you say yes.

You climb to your feet before Coach reaches you.

"You okay?" he asks.

No, not really. The pain isn't too bad now, but it feels like it could get worse.

"Yep," you lie. "Just surprised me, that's all."

Your coach looks at you, eye to eye. "You sure?"

You don't want to come out of the game, and you know that's what he's really asking. If you tell him you're fine, he'll let you play. If you say that you're hurt or even that you're worried about your shoulder, he'll sit you on the bench. Your day will be done. Should you play and help your team win? Or is it better to sit out and rest your arm? What will you choose to do?

ABOUT THE AUTHOR

Lisa M. Bolt Simons has been a teacher for more than 20 years, and she's been a writer for as long as she can remember. She has written more than 20 nonfiction children's books, as well as a history book, *Faribault Woolen Mill: Loomed in the Land of Lakes*, and she is currently working on several other projects. Both her nonfiction and fiction works have been recognized with various accolades.

In her spare time, Lisa loves to read and to scrapbook. Originally from Colorado, Lisa currently lives in Minnesota with her husband, Dave, and she's the mom of twins, Jeri and Anthony. She was a busy sports mom for over a decade.

CONFIDENCE:

SKILL:

SPEED:

TEAMWORK:

TALENT POINTS:

CONFIDENCE:

SKILL:

SPEED:

TEAMWORK:

TALENT POINTS:

CONFIDENCE:

SKILL:

SPEED:

TEAMWORK:

TALENT POINTS: